WILLIAM—THE GLOBETROTTER

William—that happy young ruffian—has delighted millions of readers over many years. The adventures recorded in this volume have appeared in print before, but not recently.

The first story, *William—The Globetrotter*, appeared in early editions of WILLIAM—THE SHOWMAN. *William and the Four-forty* and *Cats and White Elephants* were in original editions of WILLIAM—THE BOLD; *William's Secret Society* appeared in WILLIAM AND THE TRAMP; *The Pennyman's Hand on the Torch* appeared in WILLIAM THE BAD; and *William and the Over-Ten Club* appeared in WILLIAM AND THE MOON ROCKET.

Also available in an Armada edition is WILLIAM—THE ANCIENT BRITON. Two more William books will appear later in Armada. Look out for them!

William—The Globetrotter was first published in the U.K. in 1965 by May Fair Books Ltd, Dorset House, 13a Old Burlington Street, London W.1, and was printed in Great Britain by Love & Malcomson Ltd, Brighton Road, Redhill, Surrey, England.

RICHMAL CROMPTON

William—
the Globetrotter

COVER ILLUSTRATION
BY PETER ARCHER

ARMADA
PAPERBACKS
for Boys & Girls

William the Globetrotter

WILLIAM sat on a stile, his elbows on his knees, his chin in his hands, sunk in gloomy thought. Everything he had undertaken lately seemed to have gone wrong.

He had entered upon his last undertaking with high hopes. It had seemed an excellent and easy means of making money, and William, who, like most people, found his income insufficient to meet his needs, was always on the look-out for an easy means of making money.

He still considered that it was a good idea in itself, and that its failure was due simply to bad luck.

In the neighbourhood of William's home there were several mansions—chiefly Elizabethan—that were open to the public on certain days of the week. The public paid a shilling or two shillings, as the case might be, and for that sum were escorted over the mansion by a guide and bidden to mark its beauties and points of interest.

William did not see why this system should be confined to the stately homes of England. His own home, though comparatively lacking in stateliness, contained some undeniable points of interest.

There was the hole that Jumble had made in the hall carpet (now covered by a rug), the baluster that had had a piece knocked out where William had lost control in sliding down, the frog that he had (not very successfully) stuffed, the damp patch in the bathroom wall where a pipe had burst, and the attic where one could get out on to the roof or make ghostlike noises by shouting into the water cistern.

William, of course, realised that these were not equal in general interest to priests' holes and carved corbels and picture galleries and tapestries, but he considered that they *were* definitely interesting.

He did not intend to charge two shillings or even one shilling for entrance. He thought that a steady flow of visitors at a penny each, one or two afternoons a week, would prove a pleasant and easy source of income.

He did not for a moment expect that his parents would agree to this, but he did not see why they should know anything about it. His mother went every Wednesday afternoon to help at a Welfare Centre, and he thought that if he threw the house open to the public during the hours of her absence no possible harm could be done.

With vague memories of a recent visit to a neighbouring Elizabethan manor, he imagined himself conducting a small orderly party of sightseers from room to room, explaining the points of interest, answering a few timid questions, and finally ushering them out of the front door again.

Perhaps some of them would even give him a tip. He'd be able to buy that football that he'd seen in Hadley as well as the motor boat. He might get as much as five shillings a week by it. He couldn't think why he hadn't tried it before. . . .

The next Wednesday afternoon he waited till his mother had safely departed for her Welfare Centre, then fetched from his bedroom the notice that he had printed the night before on a page from his arithmetic exercise book, 'Open to the Publik Wensday Afternoon Entrunce one penny,' and hung it on the gate. That done, he took his seat by the drawing-room window to watch for clients.

6

Even now, of course, the coast was not quite clear. The visitors must not ring the bell, for, if they did, the housemaid would answer it and summarily send them about their business. William, therefore, had left the front door ajar, so that he could intercept them before they reached it and, after collecting their pennies, start the sightseeing tour. He held a small tin in which to collect their fees and sat with his eyes fixed on the gate reciting his lecture to himself. "Under this rug you see a hole in the carpet made by Jumble. There was a sort of rose in the pattern and he kept trying to get it out. I knocked that bit off the balusters with my head. I made a jolly big lump on my head—nearly as big as a football. I got how to stuff that frog out of a book. They always smell a bit. You can't help it . . ."

Quarter of an hour passed; half an hour passed. Only two people came along the road, and neither of them stopped to read the notice. William became bored. He decided to go for a walk, and, whistling for Jumble, set off by the side door, quite forgetting that the front door was still ajar and the notice still on the gate. He was away longer than he had meant to be and returned to find the place in an uproar, his mother distracted. A passing tramp had obeyed the notice, entered by the open front door, and departed with the silver vases from the drawing-room mantelpiece, duly leaving a penny on the hall table. In vain did William protest his good intentions, his desire to restore the fortunes of his family and make them all millionaires. His excuses were brushed aside and retribution sternly dealt out to him.

And that led to Miss Milton. If it hadn't been for the affair of the tramp, his mother would not have insisted on his joining Miss Milton's Educational Play Guild.

Miss Milton was one of those unfortunate beings who are cursed with a social conscience. She was always devis-

ing schemes for the betterment of mankind, and failure
only spurred her on to further efforts. Her recent agitation for the adoption of poor families by well-to-do ones
had proved a signal failure, but Miss Milton was not dis-
couraged. Far from it. She at once set to work to devise
further schemes. The latest was the Educational Play
Guild for Children.

It was to be held on Wednesday afternoons, and Mrs.
Brown immediately enrolled William, on the grounds that
then, at any rate, she'd know what he was doing while
she was at the Welfare. William protested passionately
against this.

He didn't want to be educated. He was educated every
day in school, wasn't he? Well, it wasn't fair on the
masters in school to start messing about with his education out of school. He'd be getting on too fast for them,
and then there wouldn't be anything else left to teach him,
and he'd have to leave school because of knowing everything, and then she'd have him at home all day for the
rest of his life, and how would she like that? And, anyway, he didn't want to play—not like that. He didn't
believe in mixing up play and education. He didn't think
it was right. And he didn't like Miss Milton. He never had
and he never would. And he didn't want to go to her
rotten old play guild. But it was all in vain.

With frequent references to the silver vases Mrs. Brown
remained firm in her decision. William was to attend Miss
Milton's Educational Play Guild. All verbal persuasion
having proved useless, William turned his attention to the
symptoms of various diseases, but his mother was
accustomed to this, and, the more realistic his per-
formances, the less was she impressed.

The next Wednesday, therefore, William, washed and
brushed and dressed in his best suit, was delivered by
Mrs. Brown at the Village Hall, the head-quarters of the

Educational Play Guild, on her way to the Welfare. She was to call for him on her way back. It was, she considered, providential that the Village Hall lay on her way to the Welfare. After those silver vases, she'd never have known a moment's peace at the Welfare again with William ranging at large . . .

A small party of depressed-looking children were assembled in the hall. Most of them had been sent by the parents under stress of the same emotions as had inspired Mrs. Brown. If they were in the Village Hall, being educated by Miss Milton, at least they couldn't be anywhere else doing anything else. Miss Milton was bright and alert, her eyes shining with purpose. This, she felt sure, looking at the glum faces around her and mistaking their glumness for earnestness, was going to be the most successful of all her philanthropic schemes.

"Now, children," she said briskly, "the first thing we're going to play at is Birds and Flowers. Each of the boys will be a bird and each of the girls a flower. You'll have a lovely game, and at the same time learn all about the beautiful bird and flower kingdoms."

She proceeded to assign various birds to the boys and various flowers to the girls. William received the news that he was a tom-tit without enthusiasm. Without enthusiasm also he received a detailed description of his appearance and habits. He was, he was told, a valuable destroyer of pests, fond of fat and coconut. He did not emigrate. He nested in any convenient hole near the house or along the lanes, using moss, wool, hair and feathers. His tail and wings were blue, his back a yellowish green. His song lasted all the year round.

William listened to all this with a glassy stare. Miss Milton went on to the others and told them, one by one, their characteristics as birds and flowers. She then gave them little cards with their characteristics written down.

9

"And now we'll have a jolly game," she said brightly. "I'll give you five minutes to learn what's in the cards, then I'll pin the cards on your backs and you can go round and ask each other questions about the bird or flower you represent and look on the back to see if the answers are right. Won't that be fun?"

"Yes, but what's the game?" asked William.

"That *is* the game, dear," said Miss Milton patiently. "Think what fun you'll have asking each other questions and then seeing if the answers are right! And there's another thing that I'm going to tell you. Something *very* exciting indeed, so exciting that I really don't think I ought to tell it to you just on top of the new game." She made a pause in which anticipation was supposed to stretch itself on tenterhooks, then continued. "I thought that later on we'd have a little party for your parents, to show them what jolly times we have, and you could all dress up as the birds and flowers you represent and each say a little rhyme."

"What rhyme'll I say?" demanded William.

"Well," said Miss Milton modestly, "I haven't got everything quite planned out yet, but I did think of a nice little rhyme for tom-tit.

" 'About the garden I do flit,
         Tom-tit am I, I am tom-tit.' "

William considered this in silence for a few moments, then said:

"If I've gotter be a bird, I'd sooner be a vulture than a tom-tit."

"Why, dear?" said Miss Milton.

"I'd sooner be a bird that eats dead men than one that jus' eats coconuts."

Miss Milton blenched.

10

"I don't think that's very nice, dear," she said faintly.

"I'd sooner be a vulture than any other sort of bird," insisted William. "They know when people are dyin' an' they hover round 'em an' then swoop down an' start eatin' 'em straight away. I'd like to do that. It'd be a jolly sight more excitin' than singin' in gardens an' suchlike."

"Don't, dear," said Miss Milton. "I think that's horrid. No, you're a dear little tom-tit, and you've got a dear little rhyme to say about yourself."

"I bet I could make up one jus' as good about a vulture," said William. He was silent for a moment, staring thoughtfully into the distance, then: "Yes, I knew I could. I'm jolly good at makin' up po'try.

"'I swoop right down on 'em, and then
Dead men I eat, I eat dead men.'"

"No, William," said Miss Milton very firmly, "we won't have any more of that. It isn't nice at all. It really isn't. You ought to try and fill your mind with beautiful thoughts, William——"

"Well, a vulture *is* a beautiful thought," persisted William. "It's a jolly sight beautifuller than a tom-tit any day."

"We won't talk any more about that for the present," said Miss Milton. "Let's talk about our future arrangements. I thought that perhaps next week we might each choose a great character in history, find out all we can about him or her, and tell each other. That will be great fun, won't it?"

She smiled brightly round the assembly. No one spoke except William who said:

"Mine's Guy Fawkes."

"But he wasn't a good man, dear," said Miss Milton.

"He was the only one that did *us* any good, anyway,"

11

said William firmly. "He started bonfires an' fireworks, an' that's a jolly sight more than any of the others did. Messin' about with wars an' rebellions an' things, an' never thinkin' of anyone but themselves! He thought of givin' other people a bit of pleasure, anyway. I bet he got jolly bored himself in November thinkin' Christmas was never comin', so he started fireworks an' things to cheer people up, an' I think it was jolly kind of him."

"But, William," said Miss Milton, "you're quite wrong. You——"

"I'm goin' to have him, anyway," interrupted William, "an' I bet I can make up a piece of po'try about him, too." Again he considered for a moment then: "Yes, I knew I could.

" 'You can make my moustaches with burnt corks,
    Guy Fawkes I am, I am Guy Fawkes.' "

"Nonsense, William," said Miss Milton, who was beginning to regret having put her poem about the tom-tit into that particular form. "Well, I think perhaps we won't have historical characters, after all. We'll have we'll have adventurers. Each of you must choose someone who'd had some great adventure and tell each other all about him or her next week. Now we'll go on with our bird and flower game."

An hour or so later Mrs. Brown collected a dejected boy from the Village Hall.

"We've had such a jolly time," Miss Milton assured her brightly, "haven't we, children?"

A groan, which she took to be a murmur of assent, broke from the little assembly.

"This time next week, then," went on Miss Milton. "And all get busy with your adventures."

William set off moodily homeward beside his mother.

"I'm so glad you've enjoyed it, dear," said Mrs. Brown.

"Enjoyed it?" echoed William indignantly. "Enjoyed it? Me? Enjoyed it? It's been awful. All about tom-tits and stuff. It's jus' about turned me sick. If I've gotter go there every Wednesday afternoon I—well"—darkly—"I shun't be surprised if I died."

"Nonsense," said Mrs. Brown, "and anyway, William, after those vases——"

"Those vases!" echoed William. "I'd rather've gone to prison for 'em straight off. *She* wouldn't've been there anyway, goin' on about tom-tits an' things. I wouldn't've minded goin' to prison. It'd've been fun filin' my way out with a file or diggin' an underground passage out same as people in books. 'Sides, you go on as if *I'd* stolen the vases. I don't see how I can help other people stealin' things when I'm not even there to stop 'em. I s'pose you think everythin' in the world that's stolen's my fault jus' 'cause I wasn't there to stop it. Well, come to that, it's everyone's fault, so why shun't everyone that doesn't steal be put in prison 'cause they've not been able to stop people stealin' same as I couldn't? Then that'd jus' leave thieves out of prison an' what sense is that?"

"William, dear," said Mrs. Brown mildly, "I don't know what you're talking about, but you do talk the most dreadful nonsense."

"It's not nonsense," said William. "Have I to go nex' Wednesday?"

"Of course," said Mrs. Brown. "I expect you'll get to like it when you get used to it."

"Why should I?" challenged William. "You might jus' as well say people'd get to like poison if they got used to it. They'd get to like it when they're dead, p'r'aps," he continued with heavy sarcasm, "an' that's the only way I'll get to like her an' her ole tom-tits."

13

They had reached home now, and Mrs. Brown, who hadn't been listening to him, said, "Yes, dear," vaguely, "and don't forget to wipe your feet on the mat."

William snorted defiantly but wiped his feet on the mat, washed his hands and face, and made an excellent tea.

He had meant to show his scorn of the whole proceeding by refusing to give any thought to the subject of adventure, but it was a subject that had always attracted him, and he found his thoughts turning to it despite himself.

"Mother," he said suddenly, "what d'you think's the greatest adventure that's ever been done?"

Mrs. Brown considered.

"Well, I don't know, dear. What about the discovery of America?"

"No, I don't think much of that," said William, as he thoughtfully munched a piece of bread and jam. "Whenever I do try chewin' gum I'm always swallowin' it by mistake, an', anyway, it's only made more dates to learn."

"Well, then, the discovery of the North Pole."

"No, I don't think much of that, either. They jus' went to a place that was there all the time. Anyone could do that. An' it wasn't any use when they got there—all snow an' ice an' stuff. No, I don't think much of that."

"Well, that's all I can think of," said Mrs. Brown firmly, "and, William dear, do try to eat more slowly. It's not good for you to bolt your food like that."

"Well, I've gotter keep my strength up after an awful afternoon like that, haven't I?" William justified himself, stretching out for the last piece of bread and jam. His mind was still busy with the subject of adventure, but he could think of none that really interested him.

"What about aeroplanes?" said his mother.

"No," said William bitterly, "they look like birds an'

14

"William, dear," said Mrs. Brown, "do try to eat more slowly."

I'm sick of birds. 'Tom-tit I am,' " he quoted with an expression of nausea.

That evening, however, he happened to pick up a library book of Robert's and was soon absorbed in it, deaf and blind to everything around him. It was about a man who had travelled ten thousand miles with two ponies from Buenos Aires to New York, beset by danger on every side—crocodiles, electric eels, vampire bats, and fever. It was the sort of adventure in which William's soul

15

delighted—one man pitting himself alone against gigantic hostile forces.

"Here! Give me that!" said Robert, snatching the book out of his hand indignantly, for it seemed to lower his, Robert's, dignity that a kid like William should read and enjoy his book.

"*Gosh!*" said William, still bemused by the spell of the book. "Fancy him doin' all that! Two an' a half years at it too! An' all alone! Wasn't it a wonder he wasn't killed?"

"Shut up and mind your own business," said Robert, sitting down and burying himself in the book.

William was not at all abashed by the rebuff, for it was Robert's usual mode of address to him and any other sort would have embarrassed both of them.

"I bet he felt a bit scared leadin' those ponies across those swayin' bridges over canyons," went on William.

Robert, deep in the book again, made no answer.

William spent that evening in a sort of dream. That was the adventure for him—to go ten thousand miles through the dangers of desert and jungle all alone but for his faithful ponies.

Already he was beginning to feel that he, and not the author, had performed the feat. Anyway, if one person could do it, another could. Two and a half years. Well, that wouldn't matter. If he was away two and a half years, at any rate he'd miss school and that awful stuff of Miss Milton's on Wednesday afternoon. That alone would be worth being away two and a half years. Yes, he'd do it. It was an adventure after his own heart. It would need a little adjusting, of course. He couldn't very well go from Buenos Aires to New York, as he wasn't at Buenos Aires to start with. And he might find it difficult to get two ponies.

Still, William was not the boy to give up a perfectly good plan because of a few initial difficulties. He'd take Jumble instead of the two ponies. Jumble, being only a small dog of highly mixed breed, could not, of course, serve the same purpose as the ponies, but he'd be company. And he wouldn't bother to carry tents or anything like that. He'd sleep in barns and under hedges like a tramp. He'd often thought he'd like to try being a tramp. The more he considered the project, the more alluring it became.

The money, of course, would be a difficulty, because he'd only got twopence halfpenny, and even William's optimism didn't think that that would take him far, but again, like a tramp, he would beg his way. He'd once read in the papers that beggars made a lot of money. Some of them even kept motor cars. Perhaps he'd come home a millionaire. And, of course, as he couldn't ride he'd have to walk, which was really better, he decided, as he could go across country and over fields, whereas, if he'd had ponies, he'd have had to keep to the road. For, since he couldn't ride from Buenos Aires to New York, he'd decided to walk round the world. He'd walk round the world with Jumble. It was the next best thing to riding from Buenos Aires to New York with two ponies. It seemed even to have some points of superiority.

He didn't know quite how many miles it was round the world, but more, he was sure, than ten thousand. And he'd be walking instead of riding, so it would take even longer than he'd have taken riding. Perhaps about five years. Well, he wouldn't mind being away for five years.

He'd miss school, he'd miss (he scowled with fierce effort as he did the mental sum) two hundred and sixty of those awful Wednesday afternoons of Miss Milton's. That would be worth it alone. He'd just start off and go in a straight line and he'd get back to where he started from. Well, the world was round—wasn't it?—so it stood to reason he would. He'd come to one or two seas, of course, but he'd just have to work his way across them as straight as he could. People in books always worked their way across seas . . .

He'd work it as a cabin boy or steward or mate or something. Perhaps he'd be able to save them from pirates or discover a leak in the ship just in time. They'd be so grateful that they'd make him Captain. He had a glorious vision of himself standing on a bridge, issuing orders or training his cannon on to a black ship with the skull and cross-bones flying from the mast. Then he'd sail to some undiscovered island and find a lot of hidden treasure. He pulled himself up sharply. He must stick to the adventure in hand. He was going to walk round the world, not sail to discover hidden treasure. That could come later . . .

He spent the next morning collecting his things—a compass that he'd once got out of a cracker and that would help him to steer a straight course, a penknife with something for getting the stones out of horses' hoofs that he had always felt would come in useful sometime, some dog biscuits for Jumble, his bow and arrows (he might, he thought, with luck, kill a rabbit or hare and anyway, they'd be a defence against wild animals), a length of string, some marbles and a piece of putty, because he'd had them in his pocket for so long that he'd have felt lost without them.

He made a particularly large and heavy lunch, as it might be the last square meal that he'd have for several years, then, waiting till his mother was safely lying down and the cook and housemaid busy in the kitchen, crept round the larder to forage for a few provisions. They could hardly grudge him that, he thought, considering that

18

they wouldn't have to pay anything more for his food for five years.

He filled a large paper bag with a mixture of apple pie, cold meat, breakfast sausage, cold potato, blanc-mange, and currant cake. It would, he imagined, be enough for the first few days. Then he'd have to begin begging his way.

He took a last look at his home, feeling a little wistful at the thought that it might be many years before he saw it again. The wistfulness of this thought was mingled with jubilation, however, for when he came back he'd be famous and they'd have to treat him a bit different. Even Robert would have to be polite to him. He couldn't imagine Robert being polite to him, but the fact remained that people *would* have to be polite to someone who'd walked round the world. There'd be no going to that awful thing of Miss Milton's any more. They'd be jolly sorry they'd ever made him.

"Come on, Jumble," he said and set off, feeling somewhat regretful at not having a more dramatic departure. He'd like to have had his whole family weeping on the doorstep, but, of course, if they'd been there they wouldn't have wept and they'd have stopped him going, so he realised that that was impossible. Jumble, of course, did not know that he was leaving home on a glorious adventure and behaved in his usual undignified fashion, snapping at flies, romping over flower-beds and worrying William's shoe-laces.

William walked a little way down the road and then stood, considering the situation. There were two stiles on either side of the road exactly opposite each other. It was obviously the place to begin. He'd start out by one stile and then in five years' time or so he'd come back by the other. Well, he'd have to if he went straight round the world, following his compass as he meant to.

He set his compass at the stile on the left and set off across country. He walked over the field, through a hole in a hedge and across another field, keeping in a straight line. He managed this for some time, and at last began to feel tired and hungry, so sat down under a hedge and opened his bag of provisions. He'd meant them to last several days, of course, but he might as well make a start on them now. It would make the bag less heavy to carry and help to keep his strength up. He'd only just eat a very little.

He ate absently, giving bits to Jumble occasionally, his thoughts far away in a pleasant dreamland in which he wrestled successfully with crocodiles, electric eels, tigers, lions, and returned to his native land amidst the plaudits of his countrymen. He gave a start as his eyes fell upon the empty bag. Gosh! He'd eaten it all. He hadn't meant to. Well, he'd just have to start begging his way when he got hungry again, that was all. He'd be reaching the sea soon and then he'd be a cabin boy or something, and they'd give him his food.

It must be jolly late. He'd been walking for hours and hours. Funny it wasn't getting dark. A church clock startled him by striking three. Crumbs! Only *three*. He'd thought he must almost be at the sea by now. The old church clock was probably wrong. He gave Jumble his dog biscuits, got up, and set off again, Jumble trotting happily at his heels. He'd go on a bit longer. He'd be sure to get to the sea soon.

He found himself on the outskirts of a wood, but made his way through the hedge and walked straight on. There were little nesting-boxes fastened on to the trees, and at intervals small tables, covered with nuts and crumbs of cake. William, who was feeling hungry again, cleared each as he came to it. The nuts were quite good and the cake crumbs not too stale. On one there were some pieces of

apple and these, too, William ate gratefully. There seemed
to be some providence that looked after adventurers.
Perhaps there was something in fairy tales, after all, and
he'd come under a sort of spell. He wouldn't have to
bother about begging his way, of course, if he found little
tables of food set for him all round the world.

He walked on, singing untunefully as he went. The
spell was abruptly broken by a young man with a very
pale face, nearly all nose, and a multi-coloured pullover,
who came down one of the woodland paths, carrying a
nesting-box in one hand and a coconut in the other.

"What are you doing here?" he said sternly to William.

"Me?" said William. "I'm jus' walkin' through."

He spoke coldly and distantly. The young man would
not know, of course, that he was addressing one of the
world's great heroes, one who was walking round the
entire world alone with a dog, braving innumerable
dangers.

"Walking through!" exploded the young man angrily.
"Tramping through like a herd of elephants, shouting like
a crowd of hooligans. Do you know what this is?"

"No," said William calmly.

"It's a bird sanctuary," shrilled the young man. "A
bird sanctuary. A sanctuary of peace and quiet for my
feathered friends. It's my life's work. I never come here
except in goloshes so as not to disturb them. And you—
you—come tramping and shouting—with *that*." Trembling
with rage, he pointed to the bow and arrows that William
carried under his arm. "How *dare* you come into my
sanctuary with that?"

"I'm not shootin' birds with it," explained William
patiently. "I've got it for wild beasts an' suchlike. An'
for food. In some of the places I'm goin' through I shan't
have any food except what I kill. I jolly well wouldn't
waste my arrows on birds. I've only got two an' some-

21

times when you've shot 'em it's jolly hard to find 'em again. I'm goin'——"

At this minute Jumble, who had disappeared into the undergrowth some minutes before, reappeared, leaping about excitedly and worrying a stick. The young man shrank back, white with horror.

"A *dog!*" he gasped. "A *dog* rampaging about in my bird sanctuary! The work of months undone. One of the chaffinches was nearly tame and—how *dare* you bring a dog here?"

"Well, I couldn't get two ponies," explained William, "and I've gotter have something. He'll be company in some of those wild places I'm goin' to. I've gotter go over deserts with only oases an' things to eat" (William's geography was of a somewhat scanty description) "an' over rivers full of crocodiles an'——"

But the young man was not interested in William's round-the-world tour.

"Didn't you see the notice at the gate?" he demanded.

"No, I didn't come in by the gate," explained William. "You see, I can't go round by gates an' things. I've gotter go straight on or I'll not come back to the place I started from. Stands to reason, doesn't it? When I come to houses an' places I can't get straight through, I'll have to go round 'em, of course, but places I can get through, same as hedges an' woods an' suchlike, I have to. It's goin' to take me years an' years, anyway, so I can't go wastin' my time readin' notices an'——"

"*Will* you be quiet?" snapped the young man, struggling desperately against the turgid tide of William's eloquence. "I don't know what you're talking about and I don't care. All I know is that you're trespassing on my land and disturbing my bird sanctuary, and if you aren't gone in two minutes I'll send for the police. Now get off

22

"How dare you come here with that bow and arrow?"

with you! There's the gate." He pointed in the direction from which William had come.

"I can't go that way," explained William patiently. "That's the way I've come. I've gotter go straight on same as I told you. Well, I *was* goin' straight on if you'd not come, interruptin' me an' wastin' my time. I'd've been miles on by now if it'd not been for you. Anyway, I've got as much right in a bird sankcherry as anyone, 'cause I'm a sort of tom-tit. But I wouldn't stop in it now, not even if you asked me. Come on, Jumble."

He walked on his way with stolid dignity, Jumble trotting at his heels. The young man stared after him, helpless and open-mouthed, then tiptoed along to the bird tables and stood gazing down at their empty surfaces with a seraphic smile.

Meanwhile William plodded on through the wood, across a field, along a lane, and down a road that seemed to be taking him in a fairly straight direction. He was thinking about the bird sanctuary. Bird sanctuary indeed! He'd always felt bitter about what he considered the undue importance given to birds. People making a fuss of them and putting out nuts and things for them all over the place. You might starve for all they cared as long as *birds* had plenty of coconuts and stuff.

He knew several elderly ladies, who would drive him indignantly out of their gardens and to whom it would never even occur to offer him refreshment, but who regularly set feeding trays and coconuts for birds. Bird sanctuary indeed! Why not a boy sanctuary? A boy sanctuary. It was a novel and intriguing idea. William set to work to plan its details. A wood entirely devoted to boys—grown-ups not allowed to enter. Tables of chocolate cream and humbugs and lollypops at intervals. Boy baths of lemonade and orange squash. Cream buns hanging from trees. Instead of nesting-boxes, toys placed

24

against all the trees—motor boats, bows and arrows, electric trains, cricket sets, footballs.

A boy sanctuary. He wondered no one had ever thought of it before. Fancy taking all this trouble all these years over bird sanctuaries and no one ever having thought of a boy sanctuary! It would be quite easy to arrange. He'd have done it himself if he hadn't just set out on his five years' walk round the world.

He almost wished he'd put off his walk till he'd tried the boy sanctuary. But no. Even the boy sanctuary couldn't compensate for those awful Wednesday afternoons with Miss Milton.

The road bent sharply round to the right. That wouldn't do. He must keep straight on. He climbed a fence and began to walk over a field. There were oats or corn or barley or something growing in it, but William couldn't help thát. He didn't mean to go round anything that he could possibly go through. He plodded on, still pondering on the subject of the boy sanctuary, Jumble frisking about among the green shoots, and had almost reached the other end of the field, when he heard an angry shout and glanced up to see a pair of gaiters and hobnailed boots descending upon him. His gaze rose from the hobnailed boots to meet the glare of a pair of angry eyes in a red whiskered face, and he recognised, too late, his old enemy, Farmer Jenks.

"Now I've got ye, ye young varmint," said the new-comer, and, seizing hold of William before he had time to dodge, pummelled him, boxed his ears, and threw him over the fence into the road.

William sat up and rubbed his head. His assailant was walking off down the road still muttering angrily to himself.

"All right," said William, "you wait! You just wait!

You'll be only too glad to let me walk over your ole fields when I come back famous."

Anyway, he'd got across the field and that was the great thing. He picked himself up, rubbed his head again, wondered whether to retrieve his cap, which had fallen where the farmer had attacked him, decided not to, as the farmer was not quite out of sight, and, calling to Jumble, who had discreetly vanished on the farmer's arrival and now came leaping out of the ditch, set off along the road that had turned another bend and was now spanning the world in the right direction.

The rain was beginning to fall, and William's spirits sank somewhat. People had been jolly rotten to him so far, driving him out of woods and throwing him out of fields. He compared his lot with that of the hero of the book—received with acclamation by the natives as he went along, feasted and fêted. They gave him food, and bands came and played under his window at night. Funny how differently people were treating him, William.

A steady drizzle had set in. He plodded doggedly on. He was cold, tired and hungry. He seemed to have been walking for days and days. Funny he hadn't got to the sea yet. England must be a jolly big island. He was almost tempted to regret having undertaken the adventure, but, having undertaken it, he was going to carry it through. Besides, if he didn't there'd be years and years and years of those awful Wednesday afternoons with Miss Milton and being a tom-tit. A church clock slowly struck four. Four. It *couldn't* be only four.

He was so hungry that if he didn't get something to eat soon he'd die of starvation. The road turned sharply to skirt a hedge that enclosed a house and garden. William stopped to consider the situation. He could skirt the house and garden like the road or he could go through the hedge and make his way across the garden, trusting to

26

luck to get through safely. A convenient hole in the hedge
decided him. He'd go through the hedge and make his
way across the garden in a straight line. No one seemed
to be about. He'd just make a run for it if he met anyone.
If he kept on wasting time going round things, he'd never
get round the world, and he didn't want to take longer
than he could help. He was jolly bored by it already. He
was having a much worse time than the man in the book
had had—knocked about by farmers and chased out of
woods and soaked with rain and starved. . . .

He made his way through the hole in the hedge and
stood looking about him. The sky was grey and overcast.
The rain was still falling. Even Jumble had lost his *joie-
de-vivre* and was looking at William in a slightly reproach-
ful manner, as if asking why he didn't either do something interesting or take him in out of the rain.

He made his way across the garden, passing a long
French window that showed a cosy lighted room with a
bright coal-fire and an old lady sitting at a table having
her tea. It looked a good tea. There was toast and bread
and butter and currant cake and chocolate biscuits.
Hardly knowing what he was doing, William approached
and stood there at the window, his nose flattened against
the glass, his eyes fixed hungrily upon the dainties on
which the old lady was feasting, while Jumble shivered
disconsolately at his heels.

Suddenly the old lady looked up and met his gaze. She
didn't seem at all surprised. It might have been quite a
usual thing to look up from her tea to find boys flattening
their noses on her window watching her. She got up and,
unfastening the catch of the glass door, threw it wide
open.

"Come in, come in," she said. "My goodness, *aren't*
you wet!"

"Yes, I am," agreed William, "but I don't mind bein'

27

wet so much." For it had occurred to him that this was an excellent opportunity of starting the process of begging his way round the world. "I wonder—I don't want anythin' you're goin' to eat—but if you've got any crusts or things left over——"

"Oh, there's heaps more than I shall want, here," said the old lady. "You'd better join me."

She went over to a cupboard, took out a cup and saucer, and drew another chair up to the tea-table.

"Sit down there," she said. "You'll soon get warm. And your poor little dog can lie by the fire."

As if waiting for this permission, Jumble stretched himself out with a sigh of relief on the hearthrug and promptly fell asleep.

"There!" said the old lady, pouring out a cup of tea. "It's quite hot still and so is the toast."

"You see," explained William, somewhat taken aback by this matter-of-fact reception and feeling that some explanation was called for, "I'm walkin' round the world with a dog. I'd rather've been ridin' round with two ponies, only I'd not got 'em—so I'm walkin' round with a dog."

"I know," said the old lady, nodding her head understandingly. "I used to play games like that, too."

William opened his mouth to explain, with something of indignation, that this was no game, but the old lady was handing him the toast and it seemed a pity to waste time in speech, so he took the toast and proceeded to make an extremely hearty meal. The rain lashed against the window. The sky drew darker. The prospect of spending the night under a hedge seemed less inviting than ever. . . .

"I was so glad to see you there at the window," said the old lady. "I was just saying to myself, 'I wish I'd got

28

a boy to ask about it,' and then I looked up and saw you there. It seemed like Providence."

"Yes, it seemed like that to me, too," said William fervently.

"You see," went on the old lady, "I'm giving a party to some boys next Wednesday, and I really don't know the sort of thing they like. I want you to advise me." She took a piece of paper from a table near. "We'll make a list of food together when you've finished. And you can tell me the games you think they'd like, too."

William agreed through a mouthful of plum cake.

"You see," said the old lady again, still more confidentially, "it's because of my niece, really. She's been having a sort of class for boys on Wednesday afternoons. I don't quite know what it is, but they all have great fun and these boys love it. She's only been doing it for quite a short time, and now she's taken on the secretaryship of something or other and that means she'll have to give up these boys. Well, she's terribly disappointed, as you may imagine, at having to give it up. And, of course, the boys will be still more disappointed. In fact, she said that she didn't know how she was going to break it to them, so I suggested that she should have a party for them—just to cheer them up, you know—and as her house is rather small, I said she'd better have it here and that I'd arrange it all for her, because she's so very busy with this new work. What's the matter, dear?" for William was staring at her open-mouthed, everything else, even the chocolate biscuits, forgotten.

"W-w-w-what's her name! " he stammered.

"Miss Milton," said the old lady.

"An'—an'—an' is she goin' to have all these boys to the party?"

"Yes, dear, of course she is. Just to comfort them a little for having to give up these delightful classes. I thought it would be such a good idea. A little treat does so help to tide over a disappointment, doesn't it? She's going to go round to them all this evening and break the news to them and invite them to the party. So, if you've quite finished, dear, you can help me with the list."

Half an hour later William, warm and fed and comparatively dry, set off jauntily from the front door with Jumble at his heels. The rain had stopped, but William did not continue his course round the world. He had decided to abandon it for the present. There wouldn't be any sense in missing the party for which he had just drawn up such an adequate list of refreshments and entertainment. Besides, there wasn't much point in going away now that the hated Wednesday afternoons were coming to an end. What he'd tried of walking round the world he quite definitely hadn't enjoyed. Perhaps it would be better to wait till he was older and could get two ponies. Perhaps people would treat him a bit better if he was older and had two ponies, same as they did the man in the book. . . .

He had plenty of other plans in his mind. He'd like to have a shot at a boy sanctuary and charge admission and see if he couldn't make a bit of money that way. After all, it would be an awful waste of time taking five years walking round the world.

"Hurry up and get tidy, dear," said his mother as soon as he reached home. "Your tea's ready."

William entered the dining-room and looked with dispassionate scorn at the plateful of bread and jam on the table. Nice fare that for a hero who'd just walked round the world! He bet the other man hadn't been given bread and jam when he got home. Still, he'd had quite a brisk walk since his tea with the old lady and, though he would have liked to show his scorn of the fare so unfit for a hero by refusing to partake of it, there was no doubt that bread and jam was better than nothing. He took a piece and bit into it. Mrs. Brown touched his shoulder tentatively.

"There, William!" she said reproachfully. "Your coat's quite damp. I do wish you'd be more careful. Surely you could have taken shelter during that shower."

"Huh!" ejaculated William significantly. "You can't bother about a little thing like rain when you're walkin' round the world. You're jolly lucky to have me back at all."

"What do you say, dear?" said Mrs. Brown absently.

William wondered whether to tell his mother of his heroic exploit (for by now he was almost convinced that he actually had walked round the world) but decided not to. She probably wouldn't listen to him and it would only be a waste of time.

As he reached out for another piece of bread and jam he saw the figure of Miss Milton coming up the drive. . . .

William and the Four-forty

" JUS' our luck if it's gone," panted William.

"I bet it won't have," panted Ginger. "Hi! Don't run so fast. I can't keep up with you."

"Well, don't talk so much," said William. "You oughter save your breath for runnin' same as me. I'm not talkin' all the time. I'm savin' my breath for runnin'."

"You've never stopped talkin' since we started," Ginger reminded him. "Anyway, we're nearly there now.

31

I say! Let's pretend there's a pack of wolves after us. That oughter make us run quicker."

"I'm not scared of wolves," said William. "I bet if wolves were after us I'd jus' turn round an' kill 'em one after the other."

"You've got nothin' to kill 'em with."

"I'd strangle 'em. I've got jolly strong hands. I can unscrew tops of tins an' things what my mother can't."

"You'd find a wolf jolly diff'rent from the top of a tin. Let's pretend ole Jenks is after us, then."

"Gosh, yes!" said William, putting on a final spurt, as the vision of the large angry farmer on whose grounds they were wont to trespass presented itself to his mental gaze. "I'm a jolly sight more scared of him than I am of wolves."

The final spurt landed them in front of the windows of the Hadley junk shop and there they stood, gasping for breath, their eyes fixed on the magnificent penknife that lay between an incandescent gas bracket and a rusty bird-cage with most of the bars missing.

"It's still there," said Ginger. "Gosh! It's still there. I was afraid ole Hubert Lane'd've bought it."

"An' it's still five shillin's," said William.

Every day for the past week William and Ginger had come in to Hadley to glue their noses against the window and gaze in rapture at the penknife. Although they had not five shillings between them, or, indeed, even the smallest fraction of one shilling (for various misunderstandings with the adult members of their families had in each case led to a temporary stoppage of pocket money), they felt every day a fresh thrill of relief and excitement at seeing the penknife still holding pride of place in the centre of the window.

"We might get some money, you know," William had said hopefully only the day before.

"How?" Ginger had challenged him.

"Well . . . someone might die an' leave us some."

"Who?" Ginger had challenged him again.

"Dunno," William had said a little irritably. "People do in books. I once read a tale where a boy helped an ole man over the road an' the ole man died an' left this boy a fortune."

"Well, you've never helped anyone over a road."

"No, but I helped a poor ole lame woman on to a bus las' week."

"Yes, an' you nearly pushed her over doin' it. She was jolly mad at you."

"Well, she may've repented on her death bed for callin' me all those names an' left me a lot of money."

"She didn't look the sort of woman who'd repent even on her death bed. Anyway, we've not got any money, an' we're not likely to have."

But he was wrong. For Aunt Florence had come over to spend the night at William's home and, on her departure this morning, had given him five shillings. It had been an unexpected windfall (for Aunt Florence was the vague sort of visitor who is apt to leave everything behind her except a tip), and for that reason doubly welcome. Immediately on receiving it, William had collected Ginger, and the two had set off at a breakneck pace into Hadley. Habit was so strong that, though the five shillings now reposed safely in William's pocket, they stood for a few minutes, as usual, gazing at the treasure through the window.

"Four blades!" murmured William ecstatically.

"An' a corkscrew!" said Ginger.

"An' a thing for takin' stones out of a horse's hoof," said William.

"That's not much good without a horse," said Ginger.

In William's eyes, however, that particular gadget was the high light of the whole thing.

33

B

"You never know when you'll get a horse," he said, "an' you never know when it'll get a stone in its hoof. I bet that thing might save our lives some day. . . . Anyway, I wish you'd stop breathin' on the glass. I can't see it prop'ly."

"We'll get a good laugh over ole Hubert," said Ginger, removing his breath to another part of the window-pane. "He's been crowin' over us all week an' sayin' he was goin' to buy it an' he won't have a chance now."

They stood for a few more moments gazing at the treasure and suddenly became aware that another boy had joined them.

"Hello," said the fat slow voice of Hubert Lane. "Comin' to do your spot of daily sight-seeing?"

"Yes," said William triumphantly, "an' we're goin' to do more than sight seein' to-day. We're going to buy it."

Hubert's jaw dropped. From the day the penknife appeared in the shop window, he had intended to buy it—for no other reason than that he was aware the Outlaws coveted it. But he knew that they had no money and no immediate prospect of any, and he had not been in any particular hurry to make the purchase. All he had to do was to ask his mother for five shillings, and his mother had never yet been known to refuse him anything. He was unprepared for this sudden development and had come out without his purse.

"No, you're not," he said. "I am," and, before they realised what he was doing, he had opened the door and plunged into the shop.

"I want that penknife," he said to the shopkeeper.

William and Ginger followed breathlessly, pouring out incoherent entreaties and explanations.

"Can't help that," said the man shortly. "First come, first served."

"Thanks," said Hubert, grinning maliciously. "Just

34

keep it five minutes while I run home for the money, will you?"

"Now that's a different tale," said the man. "You was in first, so you gets the knife, if you've got the money. If not, it goes to these other lads."

And, in spite of Hubert's protests, he handed the knife over to William in return for Aunt Florence's five shillings.

The three went out together. Hubert's face wore an angry scowl, the faces of William and Ginger exultant grins. William, unwisely, began to perform a dance of triumph on the pavement, in the middle of which Hubert's foot shot out, and William, his dance coming to an untimely end, fell headlong into the gutter. When he picked himself up, Hubert was a dot upon the horizon.

"All right," said William, brushing himself down with a few perfunctory gestures. "All right. I'll get even with ole Hubert for that. . . . Anyway, it's a jolly fine penknife, isn't it?"

They spent a few minutes examining it and testing the blades, then William, with the air of one performing a difficult and intricate operation, took several imaginary stones out of the imaginary hoof of an imaginary horse.

"I bet it's quite easy to do," he said, "an' it'll be jolly useful if ever we get a horse." He shut up the penknife and put it in his pocket. "Come on. Let's go to the railway track."

For the Outlaws had now forsaken their one-time passion, aeroplanes. Be the sky never so full of planes, they would not look up; nor would they even discuss whether it was a Lancaster Mark II or a Liberator Mark I. They had turned to an earlier delight. They had gone back to trains. Not only the different engines but everything connected with railways fascinated them—signals, signal boxes, sidings, tracks, ballast, points—anything as long as it had to do with trains.

Happy in the possession of the penknife, discussing both it and trains with an impartiality that might have confused anyone but themselves, they wandered on towards the track.

"Four's jolly good," said Ginger. "War-time ones only had two, even when you could get 'em. . . . Did you know that, when the automatic brakes go on, the brakes couplings don't bang together? There's something to stop 'em."

" 'Course I know," said William. "I've known that for years an' *years*. It's somethin' to do with air. An' the corkscrew might come in jolly useful. S'pose we were shipwrecked . . . We could open coconuts with it. It'd be a useful weapon against wild animals, too."

"We'd have to get jolly close to 'em to do anythin' to 'em with it, an' I bet they'd have done somethin' to us first. . . . Did you know those things on the wheels are called flanges?"

" 'Course I did! The points turn 'em to go in the right direction. . . . We could open tins with it, too. We might have tins of provisions that we'd brought from the ship on a raft an' we could pierce 'em open with this corkscrew. It'd be jolly useful."

They were passing a coal cart and horse, drawn up by the kerb, with no one in attendance. William threw a speculative glance over the animal.

"It looks to me as if it had a stone in its hoof," he said. "Bet I'll soon get it out. . . ."

"It'll kick you," Ginger warned him.

"Bet it won't."

He bent down and put his hand cautiously on the great hoof . . . to be seized and flung several yards away by a black-faced giant, who appeared suddenly and without warning in his rear.

"I'll 'ave the p'lice on you," he bellowed. "Monkeyin' about like that. Oughter be ashamed of yourself."

"But listen," said William, picking himself up from the pavement for the second time that morning. "Listen. I only——"

Then he decided that the black-faced giant, now advancing slowly and threateningly upon him, was the type of man upon whom reason would be wasted, so, with a "Come on, Ginger," he ran down the nearest corner, doubled round another corner and did not stop for breath till they had reached the outskirts of the town.

"Gosh!" he panted. "I bet we only jus' escaped with our lives. He's a murderer all right. Bet he's part of this crime wave that's in the newspapers. If I'd not been jolly quick he'd've got me all right an' he'd've jus' shoved my body into one of his ole sacks. I bet all those sacks on the cart were full of bodies he's murdered same as he tried to murder me. I bet that's why he got so mad at me for goin' close up, 'cause he thought I'd find out about it."

"I could see coal in most of 'em," said Ginger mildly.

"He could easy put a bit of coal on top of each," said William but without much conviction. "Oh, well"— reluctantly abandoning his theory—"whether he's a murderer or not, he's a jolly nasty-tempered man. Serve him right if he gets stuck in some wild moorland place miles from anywhere an' can't get on, 'cause of that stone in his horse's hoof. I wouldn't take it out for him now— not if he asked me to."

"There aren't any wild moorland places round here," objected Ginger.

"Oh, shut up talkin' about him," said William. "I'm sick of him. You would be too, if he'd half-murdered you same as he did me. . . . Come on! Let's go to the railway."

They reached the railway track and stood looking about

37

them. A closely-wired fence ran on either side, but the Outlaws were experts in manipulating fences.

"No one can see us, can they?" said William.

"There's that woman with a dog comin' along the embankment," said Ginger. "Let's wait till she's gone."

They stood staring with fixed blank faces at the far horizon as a tall upright woman with a hatchet face and grey hair approached them. Behind her waddled a small rotund Pekinese. The woman passed them without looking at them. The Pekinese paused for a moment to give them a fleeting glance of fastidious disdain. "Come on, Ching-Wo," called the woman, and Ching-Wo waddled off after his mistress.

William and Ginger stood gazing after them.

"That's ole Miss Surley," said Ginger. "She's a high-up writer an' she's come to Denwood to write a book an' she won't have anythin' to do with the people what live round here. I heard my mother talkin' about her."

"I know all about her, too," said William. "She's got a niece stayin' with her called Sally an' Robert met her at the tennis club an' fell in love with her. He says she's the most beautiful girl he's ever met."

"He's always sayin' that," said Ginger.

"Yes, he sort of can't help it," said William, who viewed the foibles of an over-susceptible elder brother with indulgence tempered by regret. "But axshully this one isn't bad. Only, of course, with her aunt not wantin' to have anythin' to do with people, he can't see much of her, so it makes him write po'try an' get bad tempered. . . . Oh, come on," dismissing the vagaries of an incomprehensible grown-up world, "let's go down to the railway. She's gone on now, an' there's no one about."

They scrambled through the wire fence and down the embankment to the track. There they wandered happily along, keeping a wary eye open for any railway official.

38

The horizon remained empty, however, except for the figures of Miss Surley and Ching-Wo. Suddenly William stopped.

"Gosh! What's that red thing?" He stooped to pick it up. "It's a red flag. A red flag an' a handle. Someone mus' have dropped it. Crumbs! We're jolly lucky to have found it."

"We can't jus' take it," said Ginger.

"No, but we can carry it about a bit an' then put it back where we found it," said William. "There's no harm in that. I'll have the flag an' you have the penknife and then we'll swop an' you have the flag an' I'll have the penknife."

"All right," agreed Ginger.

They walked on down the track. William waved the flag and Ginger brandished the penknife, then Ginger waved the flag and William brandished the penknife. They stopped imaginary trains with the flag. They did imaginary repairs to the track with the penknife. They discussed the intricacies of the railway system, each parading his knowledge shamelessly.

"There's a space left between the lengths of rails for 'spansion. I bet you didn't know that."

"I bet I've known that all my life."

"Pity it's only a single line. Did you know that on a single line the driver's always gotter carry a stick that there's only one of, so's there can't be a collision?"

"I bet I knew that before I could walk."

"I bet you didn't."

"I bet I did."

They had reached some points where a side line joined the main line.

"That goes to Dene quarry," said William. "It ends right up in the quarry, 'cause I've been there."

"I know it does," said Ginger. "I've been there too."

"I wish a train would come along."

"If you knew anythin' about trains at all," said Ginger crushingly, "you'd know that the four-forty's due any minute now."

"I bet I knew about that before you did."

"Oh, you did, did you?"

"Yes, I did."

William gave a sudden gasp.

"I *say*! "

"What's the matter?" said Ginger, but his eyes had followed William's and he, too, stared horrified at the points.

"Gosh! " he said. "They're set to go to the quarry."

"Yes," said William, "an' the passenger train'll be here any minute."

"B-but—crumbs! They mus' know what they're doin'."

"Oh, must they?" said William. "What about all those accidents there've been in the newspapers, all done by carelessness, same as this?"

"P'raps they want it to go to the quarry."

"Don't be silly. The four-forty's a passenger train an' it goes to Marleigh. They don't send passenger trains to the quarry."

"Well, they'll send this one with the points set like they are now."

"Yes, they'll all hurtle over to their deaths like they did in that picture we saw last week."

"*Gosh!* An' we can't do anythin' to stop it."

"Yes, we can. We can wave the red flag at it."

The idea was so staggering that for a few moments Ginger was deprived of the power of speech.

"We—we wouldn't dare," he stammered at last, "an' if we did I bet they wouldn't take any notice . . . I say! *Look!* There it is! You can see the smoke."

"Come on, then," said William.

40

They turned to give one last look at the points, still set to send the four-forty hurtling to its doom, then ran off down the line towards the distant plume of smoke. So intent were they on preventing the tragedy that they did not see the signals go up to give the train right of way or hear the click as the points behind them shifted.

They ran on, stumbling over ballast and sleepers. Suddenly the train was in sight . . . was almost upon them. Frantically William waved his flag. The train passed them, passed the points, still safely on the main line, then screamed to a stop. Heads craned from every window, the engine-driver leaned out from his cab, the guard climbed down from his van. Neither William nor Ginger hesitated for a second. There was only one thing to be done and they did it. They dashed up the embankment, through the fence, and disappeared in the direction of the woods, too much engrossed in their flight to notice Hubert Lane standing on the embankment path, staring at them open-mouthed. The guard started after them but soon gave it up. The train could not be kept waiting, the embankment was steep, the boys were nimble. He returned to the train and went along the line to the engine-driver.

"Nothing wrong, mate, is there?" he said.

The engine-driver, a large, hairy, philosophic man, spat on to the line.

"Naw," he said. "Boys at their tricks again, that's all it were. Knew it soon as I seed 'em with that flag, but you've gotter be on the safe side, like. If they was mine, I'd tan them good an' proper."

The guard returned to his van, fuming. He reported the incident to the station-master as soon as he reached the station, the station-master reported it to the police, the police told Sergeant Jones to see that a sharper watch was kept on the railway line in future, and Sergeant
41

William and Ginger dashed up the embankment

Jones said—to his cronies and with many verbal embel-
lishments—that if he had to guard the railway line as well
as make his normal beats he might as well go into a
mental home straight away.

And that, as far as the railway was concerned, was
the end.

But for William it was only the beginning.

William and Ginger did not stop to draw breath till
they reached the refuge of the old barn. There they stood
and stared at each other, their faces red with exertion and
dismay.

"The points had moved by the time it got there,"
panted William. "Did you see?"

"Yes," panted Ginger and added, "crumbs! We've done it now."

"Yes, we've done it now," said William grimly. "I bet they're searchin' the countryside for us. They'll have bloodhounds out before long, I shouldn't wonder."

"Will we be sent to prison?" said Ginger.

" 'Course we will, if they catch us," said William.

William had often enough said with airy nonchalance that he would not mind being sent to prison, but, now that the prospect seemed imminent, it brought a strange hollow feeling to the pit of his stomach.

"For how long?" said Ginger in a small voice.

"Ten years, I should think," said William.

"Gosh!" said Ginger, aghast. "We'll be over twenty when we come out. It'll be time to start lookin' for jobs."

"No one'll give us any jobs," said William. "We'll be branded as crim'nals for the rest of our lives."

"We'll jus' have to starve, then," said Ginger.

William said nothing. His spirit was weighed down by a load of guilt such as it had never known before. To a boy there is no mitigation in connection with the major offences. A murderer is a murderer, a thief a thief, a train-stopper a train-stopper. Actually he confused the incident with a picture he had once seen, in which desperadoes had held up a train and had been pursued by the sheriff and his men through several reels of magnificent Wild West scenery before they were finally brought to bay and shot out of hand.

Anyway, he now considered himself a criminal, hunted and apart, an outcast from respectable society, living in the world that appeared in flaming newspaper headlines, 'Crime on the Increase' or 'What are the Police Doing?' Already, he had no doubt, the machinery of Scotland Yard was being set in motion. Already keen-eyed, aquiline-nosed men, with little bags containing the paraphernalia of their trade—microscopes, rulers, finger-print powders—were on their way to the scene of the crime.

"What'll we do?" said Ginger apprehensively. "Shall we run away?"

"That wouldn't be any good," said William. "They've prob'ly got cordons round us by now."

"Well, I'm gettin' jolly hungry," said Ginger. "If we can't run away, shall we have to hide up in the woods eatin' berries? All the berries I've ever tried eatin' tasted rotten 'cept blackberries an' there aren't any blackberries out now."

William considered the situation. It was growing dark and a little chilly. The pangs of hunger were already making themselves felt. The thought of home and tea drew him irresistibly.

"No," he said. "It'll only rouse suspicions if we don't go home. We'd better go home an' carry on as if nothin' had happened."

44

"I hope we're in the same cell if they put us in prison," said Ginger.

William laughed mirthlessly.

"They put you in cells all by yourself in prison," he said. "An' everythin's got arrows all over it—cups an' saucers an' sheets an' table-cloths an' everythin'."

"Why?" said Ginger.

"Dunno . . . S'pose they started it in the days when the army fought with bows an' arrows an' they haven't used the stuff up yet. Anyway, I'm jolly hungry, too. Let's go home."

When William returned home, he found only Mrs. Brown and Robert at tea. Ethel was away, staying with a friend, and Mr. Brown had not yet returned from the office. It was one of William's fondest delusions that, by being quiet and unobtrusive and extremely polite, he would divert all attention from himself. It had, of course, the opposite effect. . . . To-day Robert was holding forth with such eloquence and animation that Mrs. Brown would not have noticed William at all if he had not refused a second piece of cake and passed the sugar to Robert without being asked. As it was, she threw him several glances of puzzled concern.

"Yes, she's invited me to tea on Saturday," Robert was saying bitterly. "After refusing to know anyone all these weeks, she's invited me to tea on Saturday."

"Well, that's very nice for you, dear, isn't it?" said Mrs. Brown, thinking that she must remember to give William a dose before he went to bed. He was looking, for him, almost pale.

Robert laughed harshly.

"Oh, it would be," he said. "It would be marvellous. Sally's the most wonderful girl I've ever met. It would make a difference to my whole life's happiness, if——"

"If what, dear?" said Mrs. Brown. "Are you feeling quite well, William?"

William turned on her the glassy and slightly imbecile stare with which he was wont to try to hide an uneasy conscience.

"Yes, thank you, mother," he said, then thinking that some acute and, if possible, incurable disease might save him from the clutches of the law, added: "At least, no, I'm not. I'm feeling jolly ill. I've got an awful pain in my back and in my stomach an' "—he paused for a moment, decided that it would be foolish to risk omitting any convincing illness by understatement, and went on—"an' in my legs an' in both my arms an'—an' in my head." He paused again and added simply, "I've got toothache too."

"*William!*" said Mrs. Brown incredulously.

"Yes, you tried that on last week, when you wanted to get out of doing your Latin homework, didn't you?" said Robert with the indifference to the sufferings of the young that is characteristic of elder brothers. "Well, it didn't work then, and it won't work now. As an artist, you know, you overload your canvas. A little restraint would make the picture much more effective."

"Dunno what you're talkin' about," muttered William. "I've not been to the pictures. Not for over a week. An' I don't see what canvassin's got to do with it. There isn't an election on. An' let me tell you——"

"That's enough, William," said Mrs. Brown. "I'm sorry I interrupted you, Robert dear. You were telling me about Miss Surley's inviting you to tea and saying that it would be wonderful if . . . ?"

"Oh, yes," said Robert, resuming his expression of bitterness. "It would be wonderful if she hadn't invited William too. *William*, of all people! 'Please bring your little brother,' she said. My whole future happiness may

46

depend on the impression I make on her, and I'm to take William with me!"

"Well, what's wrong with me?" said William in honest bewilderment.

Robert snorted sardonically.

"You needn't take him, you know, if you feel like that," said Mrs. Brown. "We can always say he has his homework to do."

"But I want to go," protested William. It had occurred to him that if he were at Miss Surley's, he might, by one of those threads of chance on which the fate of criminals so often depends, avoid being arrested in his own home and thus enabled—he wasn't quite sure how—to escape justice altogether. "I don't see why I shouldn't go. I've been *asked*. People don't often ask me to tea (again Robert snorted sardonically), an' when they do, I don't see why I shouldn't go."

"Oh, he'll have to go," said Robert with a bitter laugh. "It's all fixed up. And she's asked Mrs. Lane and Hubert so that William will have another little boy to keep him company. It's going to be nice for me and Sally in that mob, isn't it!"

"Hubert Lane!" said William in disgust. "Fancy anyone askin' Hubert Lane to tea!"

"I'd a darn sight sooner have Hubert Lane to tea than you," said Robert. "He doesn't eat like something out of the Zoo."

"No, he eats like something in it," said William, and was so delighted at his own wit that a bland smile overspread his countenance and the heavy weight lifted itself for a moment from his spirit. But only for a moment. Almost immediately Mr. Brown arrived, and the heavy weight fastened itself upon William's spirit once more.

Apprehensively he watched his father sit down to

47

tea, expecting every second to hear him launch into a description of the horrible crime that had been committed in the neighbourhood. Mr. Brown, however, launched into nothing but a description of the generally unsatisfactory nature of the train service from town. Then the evening paper came, and, as Mr. Brown opened it, William was again aware of the hollow feeling at the pit of his stomach. He waited with stony resignation for his father's outburst of horror. His father read on, silent and, to all appearance, unmoved.

William moistened his lips.

"Is there—is there anythin' about crime in the paper, father?" he said in a hoarse voice.

"What d'you mean, anything about crime?" said Mr. Brown shortly.

"I mean, have any—any speshul crimes been c'mitted to-day?"

"No," said Mr. Brown, "and you shouldn't let your mind dwell on such things. Very unhealthy. Comes of going to the pictures so much."

"I've not been to the pictures, not for over a week," protested William. "Are you sure—are you sure there's nothin' spechul? I mean—I mean, there isn't any—any train hold-ups, is there?"

"Of course not," said Mr. Brown testily. "Why should there be? What on earth's the matter with you?"

"It's only that I'm jus' sort of—sort of *int'rested* in crime jus' now," said William desperately. "I don't mean that I've—that I'm—I mean, I haven't—what I mean is, I'm jus' int'rested in crime same as you might be."

"Well, I'm not interested in crime," said Mr. Brown, "and, if you gave your mind to your school work instead of lurid rubbish like this, you might get better reports."

"Yes, but listen," said William. "That Latin report wasn't fair. It said——"

48

"Go and do your homework, William," said Mrs. Brown, seeing that her husband's exasperation with his younger son was reaching boiling point.

Mr. Brown returned to the City Prices with a grunt, and William sat down to do a Latin exercise that, the Latin master said the next day, would have driven him to drink if there'd been any drink to drive him to.

As William sat there, sprawled over the writing-table, his brows drawn into a frown, his tongue protruding from his lips (as it always did in moments of mental stress), guiding a pen that rained a gentle but unceasing shower of blots upon a handwriting aptly described in his report as "execrable," magnificently ignoring the rules of grammar, putting a nominative where there should have been an accusative, a genitive where there should have been an ablative, an infinitive where there should have been a future . . . his mind was busy over his immediate problem.

Evidently Scotland Yard had not yet released the details of the crime to the public. They were keeping them secret, he supposed, in order to throw him and Ginger off their guard. He had read stories in which that happened. Even now, probably, the keen-eyed aquiline-nosed men were on the scene of the crime, busy with torches and microscopes, examining the railway line, the points, the—— Suddenly he remembered the flag, and his blood froze with horror. He had thrown it down anyhow after he had stopped the train with it. It would have his finger-prints on it, and Ginger's . . . *Gosh!* His pen, seeming to share his agitation, deposited six blots in a wide circle and translated 'The Queen ruled' by 'Mensam amabas.'

He finished his homework and went to bed early. It would be too much to say that he passed a sleepless night, but he awoke at two o'clock and got out of bed to look through the window. It was bright moonlight, and he was relieved to see the garden empty of bloodhounds and detectives. . . .

His feeling of guilt had not lessened by the morning, and his heart almost stopped beating when he saw his father open the morning paper.

His eyes glued themselves to his porridge as he waited breathlessly for the outcry, "Good Heavens! Two boys held up the four-forty yesterday. Such things won't be tolerated in England." But his father merely made a few caustic references to the government, the weather and the state of the stock exchange, then folded up his paper, collected his things and set off as usual to catch his train. Scotland Yard were keeping jolly quiet, thought William. They'd probably been working on it all night. They'd probably got their bags filled with clues by now. . . .

He was putting together his school books in the hall when there came a loud double knock at the front door. Looking round desperately for escape, he plunged into the cupboard under the stairs where the brooms and brushes were kept. The postman's voice, apologising for having forgotten to bring a packet with the early post, reassured him, and he emerged, pale and dishevelled, to meet his mother's astonished gaze.

"What on earth are you doing in there, William?" she said.

William cleared his throat.

"Well, I—er—I jus' sort of thought I'd—er—jus' sort of tidy it up a bit. I thought it looked a bit sort of untidy."

Mrs. Brown gazed at him helplessly.

"What *do* you mean, William?" she said. "It's perfectly tidy, and in any case, why ever——" She dismissed the problem with a shrug and looked at the clock. "Now do hurry up or you'll be late."

William, remembering the sketchy nature of his homework, wondered whether to plead illness again, then decided that school at any rate put off his arrest for a few hours (the detectives would be sure to go to his home first) and provide a good starting point, by way of the playing fields, for a flight from justice that might take him all over the inhabited world and last for the rest of his life.

He pulled his cap low over his eyes, turned up his coat collar, hunched up his shoulders, and went down to the front gate, where he stood for a moment, looking up and down the road. No one was in sight. Slowly and cautiously he set out. . . .

The sudden emergence of a figure from a side lane set his pulses racing, but almost immediately he realised that it was Hubert Lane, and his pulses returned to normal. Rather to his surprise, Hubert seemed to be waiting for him. Oppressed by a crushing weight of guilt, haunted by fear of the law, expecting every moment to hear the distant baying of bloodhounds, William was not as yet so lost to a sense of his immediate surroundings as to forget that he owed Hubert one for tripping him up yesterday. He advanced upon him with the obvious intention of squaring their accounts. To his further surprise, Hubert did not turn to flight. Instead, he stood his ground, fixed William with a small malicious eye and said in his silkiest voice:

"Hello. . . . Been holding up any more trains lately?"

William paled. His jaw dropped open. For a few moments he stared at Hubert in speechless dismay, then he rallied his forces as best he could.

"Dunno what you mean," he said.

"Don't you?" sneered Hubert. "Fancy that! Fancy

51

you not knowing what I mean! Oh, no, it wasn't you that held up that train yesterday, was it? Fancy me thinking it was you!"

William opened and shut his mouth soundlessly.

"Well, I'm going to the police about it," went on Hubert. "I think it's my duty to go to the police. I'll tell them I saw two boys just like you and Ginger holding up that train yesterday afternoon. It'll be all right, you know. All you have to do is to prove your alibi, if it wasn't you."

William blinked.

"I—I wouldn't do that if I was you, Hubert," he said hoarsely. "I mean—I mean, they're jolly busy, the p'lice. I—I don't think it's fair to waste their time on a little thing like that."

"I thought that was what they were there for," said Hubert, taking a cat-like delight in playing with his victim. "I thought they were there for catchin' criminals and puttin' them in prison."

William moistened his dry lips.

"There've been a lot of burglaries about lately, Hubert," he said, "an' I think they're too busy over them to bother about anythin' else jus' now."

"P'raps," said Hubert. "But they could put it down on the waitin' list. I s'pect they'd soon work down to it. Say, in a week."

"I wouldn't, Hubert," said William. "Honest, I wouldn't if I was you. They they might think you did it, you know."

"Oh, no, they wouldn't," sniggered Hubert. "The guard saw those boys, you know. He'd recognise 'em all right."

William stood, his face set and frozen, staring in front of him. Hubert judged that the moment had come to draw the net more closely round the victim.

Hubert received a swipe from William

"Got that penknife on you?" he said casually.

"Yes."

"Well, let me have it, will you? I've got several things I want to do with it an' they'll prob'ly keep me so busy I won't have time to go to the police."

William hesitated a moment, then slowly, reluctantly drew out the knife. Hubert pocketed it and swaggered off, whistling carelessly to himself.

It was William's first experience of blackmail, but it was not to be his last. The next day Hubert demanded his mouth organ, and the next his water pistol. William handed them over, but he was not cast by nature for the rôle of worm and on the third day he turned. Hubert, complacently demanding his pencil sharpener, received instead a swipe in the eye that sent the enterprising youth rolling into the ditch and deprived him for some moments of the power of vision. He picked himself up and ran off, howling, but secretly he was not ill-pleased.

He had not really wanted any of William's possessions except the knife (for his parents indulged his every wish) but as long as William went on giving he felt he had to go on asking. He was tired of blackmailing. He felt that he would now get a far greater kick out of exposing William.

He decided, however, not to report the incident to the police. The police would go to Mr. Brown and the whole thing might be hushed up. No, William must be exposed in public where no hushing up was possible. His howls died away, as he began to plan his campaign, and a slow smile overspread his fat, tear-stained face.

So occupied had William been by his own misfortunes that he had completely forgotten Miss Surley's invitation till lunch-time on Saturday when his mother said: "Now, William, don't go far away this afternoon. Remember that you're going to tea to Miss Surley's with Robert."

William stared at her aghast.

"What," he said, "goin' out to tea with that ole woman? *An'* with Robert?"

"As I said before," said Robert grimly, "I shall be only too glad to dispense with your company. It's an occasion on which my whole future happiness may depend, and I've never yet known you go to tea anywhere without displaying the table manners of a hog and the tact of a rhinoceros."

This touched Mrs. Brown's maternal pride, and she rallied to the defence of her younger son.

54

"Oh, he's not as bad as that, Robert," she said. "He can behave quite well when he likes."

For answer Robert did his sardonic snort.

"You said you wanted to go, William," went on Mrs. Brown.

"Yes, I do," said William, remembering that a visit to Miss Surley had seemed to offer a temporary respite from the doom that overshadowed him. "An' anyway there'll prob'ly be a decent tea. It's ages since I had a decent tea."

Robert did his sardonic snort again.

"Why shouldn't I go, same as you?" said William indignantly. "I've gotter right. I've been *asked*."

"Yes, dear," said Mrs. Brown, "there's no reason at all why you shouldn't go if you want to. I'm sure you'll try to behave like a little gentleman, won't you?"

Robert's snort at this seemed to shake the house to its foundations.

Robert had arranged to attend a meeting of the cricket club in the village hall that afternoon and to go straight to Miss Surley's from there, so William would have to make his way to the tea-party alone. With only perfunctory protests he endured a strenuous half-hour's restoration process at the hands of his mother, emerging from it so clean and tidy, so immaculately suited and stockinged and shoed as to be almost unrecognisable. His burnished hair shone, his burnished face shone, even his burnished knees shone. His gartered stockings were creaseless, his shoe laces tied in neat bows.

Mrs. Brown saw him off at the front door, smiling proudly.

"You *do* look nice, dear," she said. "Now you've plenty of time, so there's no need to hurry."

Mrs. Brown, of course, was anxious that he should not arrive at his destination hot and sticky, but it was always a mistake to tell William that he had plenty of time.

He walked slowly and decorously down the lane into the main road, resisting even the temptation to investigate a movement in the ditch that might have been made by a water rat. His face wore the blank expression that went with his best suit. His lack-lustre eyes scanned the horizon . . . then brightened suddenly.

Round the ricks in the further corner of Three Acre Meadow he could see a crowd of men and boys and dogs. A rat hunt was evidently in progress. William stopped to consider the situation. His mother had said that he had plenty of time. There could be no harm in his just watching the rat hunt for a few minutes. He climbed the stile and set off at a run across the field.

Miss Surley was not looking forward to her tea-party. A well-known literary figure, she had taken Denwood in order to have quiet and seclusion for working on her new book, not in order to join in the social life of the village. In fact, she had made it clear from the outset that she did not intend to join in the social life of the village.

She had asked her niece Sally to stay with her in the hope that she would act as her official secretary and spare her the rude shocks and buffets of life by dealing with servants and tradespeople, turning away callers, and generally ensuring for her aunt the quiet and seclusion she needed.

But Sally, who was young and pretty, had other ideas. . . . She had managed to join the local tennis club, where a local youth, called Robert Brown, had become enamoured of her. As he was, Miss Surley gathered, the most personable youth in the place, Sally had, as a matter of course, become enamoured of him in return.

The situation irked and irritated Miss Surley, but she

could not ignore it. If Sally was going about with this local youth—and she evidently was—Miss Surley must do her duty and ask him to the house. She would ask him, she told Sally, on condition that other people were asked too, so that she, Miss Surley, might be spared the irksome task of playing chaperon. Had he a sister? Yes, but she was away from home. Had he a brother? Yes, Sally seemed to remember that he had once mentioned a young brother and then had hastily changed the subject. The young brother must come, decreed Miss Surley. And who was that tiresome woman who had called on her, though she had been careful to let everyone know that she did not wish to receive callers? Mrs. Lane, that was it. She had a small boy. They must both come. That would fulfil Miss Surley's social obligation to the tiresome woman and give the local youth's young brother a companion.

So the tea-party was arranged, and Miss Surley decided that it should be the last. She meant to freeze off the tiresome woman and the local youth so effectually that thereafter she would be left in peace.

Robert, Mrs. Lane and Hubert arrived on the stroke of four. Of William there was no sign. Robert noted this fact with mingled relief and apprehension—relief at the thought of a few minutes' respite from William's forceful personality, apprehension as to what might be delaying it.

Sally, sitting behind the tea-table, ready to pour out tea, looked adorable. Miss Surley, sitting very upright in a wing chair, managed somehow to convey the idea that she considered herself alone in the room. Mrs. Lane and Hubert, sitting side by side on the settee, smiled smugly around them. Ching-Wo, dozing on his cushion by the fire, emitted deep rhythmic snores.

Robert had taken the seat next Miss Surley and, his

lips fixed in a frozen smile, was trying to make a good impression on her. It was uphill work. He talked brightly of the weather, enquired solicitously after her health, and was met by a frigidity that would have silenced anyone but a rash and infatuated youth. Sally watched nervously from behind the tea-table. . . .

Then William arrived. . . . He had realised in the middle of the rat hunt that it was after four, and tearing himself away from the entrancing scene, had run all the way to Denwood.

He still considered that he had merely watched the rat hunt, but his face and hands were black, his hair stood up in wild disorder, mud covered his shoes and clung to his bunched stockings, for he had taken off his garters to use as catapults in one of the tensest moments of the chase.

He stood for a moment or two on the door-step, collecting his forces, then he rang the bell, gave his name and was announced by the maid, who continued to gaze at him in a fascinated manner before she finally departed.

Miss Surley shook hands with him rather gingerly, noticing with the restraint of the well-bred that clumps of moist black mud were dropping from his shoes on to her Persian carpet and that ample reserves still remained in the folds of his stockings. Robert's face was a mask of horror. . . . William, happily unaware that any change had taken place in his appearance since he left his mother's hands, muttered, "How d'you do" to Miss Surley, then sat down, placing a grimy hand on each grimy knee and gazing around with that scowling intensity that marked his company manners. Robert should have nothing to complain of *this* time, he was thinking. . . .

The maid brought in tea, returning later with brush and pan in order unobtrusively to remove the more impressive mementoes of the rat hunt. A silence fell over

58

the gathering, broken by faint titters from Hubert Lane. Robert had given up his attempt to make a good impression on his hostess. He sat, stunned and silent, amid the ruins of his life's happiness. William, still unconscious of having given any cause for complaint, sat munching chocolate cake, ignoring his fellow guests and adding an upper crust of crumbs to the mud around his feet.

Hubert, prompted by his mother, began to tell of his success at school, repeating the more gratifying comments from his half-term report.

Suddenly Miss Surley felt that she had had as much as she could stand.

"If you'll excuse me," she said rising, "I have some letters I must write. Sally will entertain you."

Hubert drew a deep breath. He saw that he had delayed almost too long. There was not a moment to be lost.

"Oh, mother," he said, "I've got something to tell you. Something dreadful."

All eyes were turned to him. William's jaw ceased its steady rhythmic munching. Only Robert, still sitting stunned amid the ruins of his life's happiness, showed no signs of interest.

"What is it, my darling?" said Mrs. Lane.

"It's about William Brown."

William swallowed a mouthful of chocolate cake unmasticated and hastily assumed the expression of vacancy with which he was wont to meet the major crises of his life.

"Hush, dear," said Mrs. Lane. "You mustn't tell tales."

"But I *must* tell you, mother. It's worrying me so. . . . William and Ginger stopped the four-forty train on Tuesday afternoon and then ran away. I don't want William

59

to be punished, but I think the police ought to be told who did it."

There was a tense silence. Even Robert emerged from his ruins to glare first at Hubert, then at William. Every face was transfixed by amazement—except Miss Surley's. For the first time that afternoon Miss Surley's face showed animation, even pleasure. She advanced towards William with hands outstretched.

"So *you're* the brave boy who stopped the train that afternoon when my little Ching-Wo got on to the line?"

William stared at her uncomprehendingly.

"You saved his life, my dear boy. Another minute and the train would have been over him. I wanted to thank you then and there, but you vanished as soon as your brave deed was performed."

"But he stopped a train," protested Hubert in a voice of anguish. "He ought to be put in prison."

Miss Surley gave him an acid look.

"I thought you didn't want him punished," she said.

Hubert's face had turned a rich shade of purple.

"You shut up! " he shouted.

"Hubert, darling! " his mother admonished him.

But Hubert was beyond restraint. His great hour had come and was covering William, not himself, with glory. He burst into noisy tears.

"We'd better go," said Mrs. Lane, rising hurriedly. "He's very highly strung, you know. Thank you for a delightful tea-party, Miss Surley."

She drew Hubert, still howling, from the room. Outside, they saw him kicking her legs.

"What a sweet child! " said Miss Surley. Her frigidity had vanished like snow in sunshine. "You'll stay to supper, won't you, Robert? I shall be too busy to entertain you, I'm afraid, but Sally will look after you. Perhaps she'll take you into the garden now and show you the outdoor study I'm having made. I'm sure you'll find it interesting."

Robert and Sally beamed at each other. . . . Miraculously, incredibly, the ruins of Robert's life's happiness were building themselves up into quite a promising edifice. They went through the french windows into the garden, so much engrossed in each other that they passed the outdoor study without even seeing it.

William, left alone with his hostess, stared first at his feet, then at the wall in front of him, then at his feet again. His face slowly darkened to brick red.

"I—I didn't see your dog," he blurted out at last.

Miss Surley looked at him, and the hatchet countenance softened into what was almost a grin.

"Actually I wasn't sure that you had done," she said, "but I *did* dislike that Lane boy so much. And the fact remains that you saved Ching-Wo's life. Have another piece of chocolate cake."

Gratefully William plunged at the cake-stand.

"Ching-Wo," said Miss Surley, "thank this kind boy for saving your life."

Ching-Wo broke off a snore mid-way to lift his silky head from its cushion, gave William a glance of ineffable contempt, then let it fall back again and continued his snore.

William's Secret Society

"IT'S rotten," said William gloomily. "They said it was comin' at the beginning of this month an' it's the middle an' it's not come yet."

"P'raps it's had a puncture," suggested Ginger.

"P'raps the lions got out an' ate up the rest of it," suggested Douglas.

"I bet the Pig with Human Brains had somethin' to do with it," said Henry. "He was jolly clever. Gosh! The way he could add! P'raps the Gov'nment borrowed him to help with the Income Tax sums or somethin' like that an' they're waitin' till he's finished."

"I bet they're not comin' at all," said Douglas gloomily. "They've never been as late as this before."

Twice a year a fair was held in the big meadow just outside Hadley, and the Outlaws were enthusiastic patrons of it. They were familiar with all the sideshows—the Lady of Lions, the Thinnest Man in the World, the Flea Circus, the Wild West Show, the Dodgems, the High Flyer, the Sky Rocket, the Super Airways and the Wall of Death—and would have been deeply outraged by any alteration.

"Gosh! It seems years an' *years* since the las' time they came," said William, thinking of the blissful evening he had spent with Professor Golightly watching the Wall of Death at Hadley Fair.

"I got a coco-nut as near as near," said Ginger. "I bet I get one quite nex' time."

"If there *is* a nex' time," said Douglas. "P'raps they've lost the map an' forgot the way."

The Outlaws walked on down the road for some time in silence. Gradually the gloom cleared from William's countenance.

"Tell you what! " he said. "Let's do somethin' excitin' ourselves to make up."

"What?" said Ginger.

"How excitin'?" said Douglas a little apprehensively.

"We'd never do anythin' as excitin' as the Wall of Death," said Henry.

62

"We won't *try* an' do the things they do in fairs," said William. "We'll do somethin' quite diff'rent. Somethin' we've never done before."

"What?" said Ginger again.

William was silent for a few moments; then, with a burst of inspiration: "We'll have a Secret Society."

"Gosh, yes! " said Ginger. "That's a jolly good idea."

"An' we'll have pass-words an' disguises," said William, "an' put up a notice an' have a meetin' in the old barn an' I'll make a speech."

"You can't make a speech about a Secret Society," said Henry. "If it's a Secret Society it's gotter be secret."

"Yes, I s'pose so," said William regretfully. He prided himself on his powers as a public orator and did not like to let slip any opportunity of using them. "Never mind. We can fix up some jolly excitin' passwords an' disguises an'—an' aliases. We'll strike terror into their hearts all right."

"Whose?" said Ginger.

"Crim'nals," said William. "We'll have a Secret Society for puttin' down crim'nals, an' I bet by the time we've finished there won't be a single crim'nal left."

"That's goin' to be jolly hard lines on judges an' p'licemen," Ginger pointed out.

"Y-yes," agreed William. "Well, we'll leave 'em just a few. They can keep some of the little ones to practise on, but we'll put down all the big ones. Now let's settle passwords an' disguises an' things."

They spent the next half-hour deciding passwords and disguises.

"There's that jockey cap Ethel wears when she goes ridin'," said William. "I bet no one could tell me from a jockey if I wore that."

"An' there's that tweed hat my father wears when he goes fishin'," said Douglas. "It's got flies stuck all over it

63

an' I bet anyone'd think I was a fisherman if I wore it."

"An' there's that hat my uncle wears when he does his bees," said Ginger. "I could pinch that an' I bet anyone'd think I was a bee man."

Henry was weighing the rival merits of his George Washington fancy dress costume (which he thought would effectively disguise him as a film star), and an overall of his mother's, irreparably stained in the making of damson jam (which, he thought, with the addition of her pastry brush, carelessly tucked in at the waist, would give him the appearance of an eminent artist) when a fall of soot in the sitting-room fireplace at home determined him to black his face and hands in a manner that would make him indistinguishable from a professional chimney sweep.

The first meeting was held in the tool-shed of Ginger's house—a cunning step devised to put off the scent such unknown enemies as might think that they would meet, as usual, in the old barn. The members made their way to the spot by devious and circuitous routes—again in order to deceive possible enemies—giving the passwords in assumed voices before they were admitted by William. The assumed voices had been the subject of lengthy discussion. Finally William had decided to speak in a deep bass voice, Ginger in a high treble, Douglas in a quavering tremulo and Henry in a short sharp bark. Douglas, who had forgotten the password ('Death to Criminals'), was refused admittance but managed to effect an entry through the window while the other three were discussing the situation.

An elaborate oath of secrecy was then administered and a still more elaborate system of signals devised by which they were to indicate to each other various degrees of danger—no danger, middling danger, special danger, deadly danger, pressing need for reinforcement and even the immediate calling in of Scotland Yard. And then suddenly things seemed to fall rather flat.

"Well, what're we goin' to *do*?" said Ginger.

"We've settled what to do," said William a little irritably. "We're goin' to put down crim'nals."

"Well, we've got to find 'em to put 'em down," said Ginger.

"An' we've got to start on one special one," said Henry. "We can't start on the whole lot together. We don't know where they live for one thing."

"They live in the underground," said Ginger.

"You're thinkin' of the underworld," said Henry. "It's somethin' quite diff'rent."

"We ought to be a bit careful," said Douglas. "They slash with razors, do crim'nals."

"I bet I'd get a crim'nal before he'd time to pull his razor out," said William. "I'm jolly strong. Look! You can feel my muscle goin' up an' down when you put your hand on my arm. Gosh! It's *enormous*."

"It's not bigger than mine," said Ginger.

"It is."

"It isn't."

"All right. *Feel* it."

"You feel mine."

The two had a spirited wrestling match in the somewhat restricted space of the tool-shed; then, refreshed and invigorated, returned to the matter in hand.

"We've got to decide what *kind* of a crim'nal we're goin' to start on," said Henry. "There's all sorts of crim'nals. There's robbers an' murderers an' forgers an' hold-uppers an' smugglers an' kidnappers an'—an' infidels an' heretics an'——"

"They're all a bit old-fashioned," said Ginger. "I'd like to start on someone a bit new-fashioneder than those."

"*Tell* you what!" said William. "There's the new sort

65

C

that go off to Russia with sci'ntific secrets. Let's catch one of them."

"Gosh, yes!" said Ginger. "That's a good idea. But"—something of his eagerness vanished—"I bet there aren't any round here."

"I bet there *are*," said William. "No one knows where they are. Well, it's news to *me*"—with his hoarse ironic laugh—"that there's anythin' about this partic'lar place that stops crim'nals comin' to it."

"What about old Stinks?" said Henry. "He's always messin' about in the lab."

Their thoughts turned to the elderly innocuous science master at the school they attended . . . and regretfully dismissed him as a suspect.

"He doesn't do anythin' but play golf an' grow chrysanthemums for the Flower Show," said Douglas.

"He's jolly old, too," said Ginger. "I bet he doesn't know anythin' about atom bombs. I bet he's still tryin' to find out how gunpowder works."

"Anyway, they find out about atom bombs in London," said William, "in places like The Tower an' the House of Commons, an' he never goes to London."

"I think we'd better be a bit careful of atom bombs," said Douglas. "They're s'posed to be dangerous."

"Anyway, I think this would be a jolly good place for an atom bomb stealer to come to," said William, " 'cause no one'd ever suspect them. Someone might find out all about atom bombs in London an' then come to a quiet country place like this to write it all down an' get it ready to take off to Russia."

"Yes, but there isn't anybody——"

They stopped and stared at each other open-mouthed.

"Mr. Kellyngs!" they said, all in the same breath.

"Gosh, yes!" said William excitedly when they had recovered from their amazement. "Fancy us not thinkin' of him! There he is, stayin' at Mrs. Barnet's at Honey-suckle Cottage an' writin' all day long. 'Course he's writin' about atom bombs an' as soon as he's finished he'll be off to Russia with it."

"An' he's got a beard, too," said William. "I *bet* he's a Russian."

"He's got a funny name, too."

"Gosh, yes! " said William. "I bet it's a Russian name. *'Course* it is. It's got s-k-y in it. All Russians names have got to end in -sky, 'cept Stalin an' he's allowed not to 'cause he's the head of the gang. This man's muddled his name up to put people off the scent, but I bet in Russia he puts the s-k-y at the end same as the rest of them."

"Yes, but he's a naturalist," said Henry mildly. "He's writin' a book about insects."

William gave another hoarse ironic laugh.

" 'Course he *says* he's a naturalist. He can't *say* he's an atom bomb stealer. They'd execute him straight away if he did."

"An' he comes from London," said Douglas. "I heard someone say so."

"Well, that proves it," said William. "He's stole atom bomb secrets from the Tower of London, an' he's come here to throw the p'lice off the scent an' so's he can write it all down quietly an' then suddenly one day he'll be off to Russia with it an'—an' we've got to stop him."

"How?" said Ginger.

"We've not got any proof," said Henry.

" 'Course we've got proof," said William; then as another idea struck him, "All right. Let's *get* proof. I'll be good practise for puttin' crim'nals down. We'll wear our disguises and use our passwords an' things an' then we'll have another meetin' this time tomorrow an' all bring the proofs we've c'lected."

He gave the complicated signal that dismissed the

"We've got to stop this black-hearted traitor," said
William

meeting and the still more complicated signal that meant
'No immediate danger', after which the Outlaws, once
more by devious and circuitous routes, made their way
home.

The meeting next day was held with elaborate secrecy.
The place of the meeting was changed from Ginger's tool-
shed to Henry's coal-shed (in order to throw off anyone
who might have discovered the former meeting place) and
the password changed from 'Death to Criminals' to 'The
Bull-dog Grip'. Douglas, who was slightly confused by

the rapid development of events, gave 'Death to Bull-dogs' as the password and again effected an unobtrusive entry while the others were discussing whether or not to admit him.

"Ladies an' gentlemen," said William, addressing the meeting in his most oratorical fashion. "I mean, gentlemen an' not ladies. Now we've all got to stop this black-hearted deadly traitor goin' off to ole Stalin with his atom bomb secrets what he stole from the Tower of London. An' we've got to have proof it's him, though we're jolly well sure it is, to start with. I bet we all got some jolly good proofs yesterday an' I bet by the time we've all told 'em we'll have enough to send him to prison an' get him executed, same as he ought to be. I got a jolly good proof, but I'll leave mine to the end. What proof did you get, Rupert of the Fiery Heart?"

Douglas, who had forgotten the name by which he went in the Secret Society and did not recognise himself under this pseudonym, continued to stare blankly at William till he realised that the gaze of everyone was focused on him and came to himself with a start.

"Oh, me!" he said self-consciously. "Well, I found a proof, all right. I heard Mrs. Barnet talkin' about him in the post office an' she said he had lemon in his tea 'stead of milk an' I know that's called Russian tea, 'cause I saw it once on one of those cards in a restaurant, so that *proves* he's a Russian."

" 'Course it does," said William. He looked at Douglas with faint disapproval. "You didn't run into much deadly danger findin' that out."

"No," agreed Douglas simply. "I didn't mean to."

"Well, what about you, Ginger? I mean Hector the Dare-Devil."

Ginger leapt to his feet.

"I got a jolly good proof," he said. "I crept up to the

69

window where he was writin'. There was a good thick bush to hide me, an' anyway I was wearin' my bee-man's hat, so, if anyone'd seen me, I could pretend I was a bee-man looking for bees, an' got so close I could see what he was writin' an' he went out of the room once, so I could put my head right through the window an'——Gosh! I could tell as plain as plain he was writin' about the atom bomb. I'd got a piece of paper an' I wrote down on it what he'd put. He'd wrote"—he took a crumpled piece of paper from his pocket and spelt the words out slowly—"Hypomma bituberculata. He was pretendin' it was the name of a spider, but there's atom bomb in it. The letters are all muddled up but there's the letters of atom bomb in it."

"There's other letters, too," Henry pointed out.

"'Course there is," said Ginger. "It's a code, you chump. He'd have to put other letters in as well as atom bomb to throw people off the scent."

"You've got to use the b twice over to make 'atom bomb' out of it," said Henry.

"That's to put people off the scent, too," said Ginger, "an', anyway, I found another one. He'd wrote down"—again he consulted his piece of paper and spelled out the words letter by letter—"Salticus scenicus, an' he was pretendin' that was the name of a spider, too, but it's got Stalin in it. S-t-a-l-i-n. 'Course he had to put other letters in, too, to throw people off the scent, but that's just his cunnin'. It's as plain as plain he was writin' to Stalin about the atom bomb secrets he'd stole."

"Yes, that's a jolly good proof," said William, "an' I did the same as you. I'll tell you what I did." He assumed his oratorical manner. "Ladies an' gentlemen. I mean gentlemen an' not ladies. Now listen to what Rudolph of the Bloody Hand—that's me—did. I went to that bush same as Hector the Dare-Devil. . . . You'd

70

William peeped in the window

jolly well messed it about, too, Hector the Dare-Devil."

"Well, p'r'aps I did," admitted Ginger. "I had to break a few bits off to see prop'ly."

"Well, there wasn't much of it left by the time I got there," said William. "Anyway, I was wearin' that jockey cap of Ethel's so's I could pretend I was a jockey what'd lost his horse in a race an' was lookin' for it, but no one

saw me an' he was writin' away like mad an' he'd got a
sort of look in his eye that'd have told me he was a
traitor after atom bombs even if I'd not known anythin'
about him. He'd just drawed somethin' on a page an' he
was writin' under it that it was a cocoon, but it was an
atom bomb plain as plain an' on the other side of the
page he'd drawed something that he'd wrote under was
a spider's web, an' as soon as I got home I looked at a
spider's web an' it was as diff'rent as diff'rent from what
he'd drawed so I know that what he'd drawed was the
inside of an atom bomb. He'd drawed the outside of it on
one page, an' called it a cocoon, an' he'd drawed the
inside on the other page an' called it a spider's web.
Gosh! He's jolly cunnin'. Then I broke another branch
of the bush tryin' to see closer, an' he looked up sudden
an' he'd got murder in his eye, so I went off quick as
quick. I only jus' escaped with my life."

"Yes," said Ginger, "he'd got a savage look about
him when I was there. I 'spect he'd stick at nothin'. I
'spect he's one of those crim'nals that'd wade in people's
blood soon as look at 'em."

"What about me?" said Henry in an aggrieved tone of
voice. "When's someone goin' to ask me what I found
out?"

"All right," said William. "I'll ask you now. . . .
Henrico the Terrible, what hast thee discovered?"

"I discovered somethin' all right," said Henry, molli-
fied by William's impressive manner, "an' I went right
into the jaws of death doin' it, too. I waited till they'd
both gone out—the crim'nal an' Mrs. Barnet—then I
went in, 'cause she'd left the door unlocked, an' I went
right into his bedroom and had a look round, 'cause I
thought I might find some atom bombs hid under his
clothes in his drawers. I'd blacked my face so's I could
pretend to be a chimney sweep havin' a look at the

72

chimney if they came back sudden. Anyway, I didn't find an atom bomb, but I jolly well found somethin'."

"What?" said the others eagerly.

"I found a waistcoat with fur on its inside," said Henry. "Well, that shows he comes from Russia. They wear clothes with fur on 'em in Russia. I've seen pictures of Russians dressed in clothes with fur on 'em, throwing things at wolves. I bet he thought no one'd notice a bit on a waistcoat an' he'd got it hid under a thing that looked like a box with shoe-cleanin' things in, but I bet it was really a secret wireless for talkin' to Stalin."

"Gosh, yes!" said William. " 'Course it was. Well, now we've *proved* he's an atom bomb stealer. I knew he was all along."

"Yes, but what are we goin' to do about it?" said Henry.

"That's what we've got to think out," said William. "I haven't quite got an idea yet, but I bet I get one soon. Tell you what we'll do first of all. We'll *shadow* him, same as they do in books; then, when we think he's ready to go off to Russia, we'll—we'll close in on him."

The others eagerly agreed. The position of having a convicted criminal under their observation was a pleasant one and they did not wish to jeopardize it by any premature action.

During the days that followed Mr. Kellyngs came to the conclusion that the juvenile population of the village was larger than he had at first imagined. Small boys seemed to hem him in on all sides wherever he went. He fell over them, bumped into them, found them at his heels, blocking his path, almost, it seemed, in his pockets. They wore strange garments, they spoke in strange voices, they called each other by strange names, but, beyond a vague feeling of exasperation, Mr. Kellyngs, busy preparing his book for the press, took little heed of them.

73

Then, one morning, William summoned a meeting of his Secret Society in the old barn.

"He's goin'," he said, forgetting his oratorical manner in his excitement. "He's goin' tomorrow. I heard Mrs. Barnet tellin' someone in the village. We've gotter *do* somethin' now an' do it jolly quick."

"What?" said Ginger.

"We've got to stop him goin'."

"How?"

"Well, Gosh!" said William irritably. "Use a little 'magination. How *do* people stop people doin' things?"

"They kidnap them in books," said Henry, "but there's lors against it."

"Well, never mind that," said William. "Stands to reason you've got to use crime when you're fightin' a crim'nal. Still"—he stopped, mentally contemplating the stalwart thick-set figure of their intended victim—"it might be a bit difficult. . . ."

"Yes, we don't want to end up bein' kidnapped ourselves," said Douglas.

"Well, we've got to decide somethin' quick," said William. "We don't want him to get off to Stalin while we're sittin' here talkin' about it."

"I bet nothin' we could do would scare him," said Ginger. "I bet that ole Stalin's the only one those ole Russians are scared of. I bet he's as big as two ordin'ry men an'——"

"No, he's not," said Henry. "There's a picture of him in our encyclopædia an' he's a little man with a sort of bushy moustache an' he wears a sort of blouse an' a porter's cap."

"*Gosh!*" said William. "I've got an idea, then. I could dress up as Stalin an' we could tell him that Stalin's come over to fetch his atom bomb stuff an' he'd come an' give it me an'—an' we'd take it up to London to the

74

gov'nment an' they'd catch him an' put him to death an' I bet everyone'd be jolly grateful to us."

"No one's ever been grateful to us yet," said Douglas gloomily.

"It won't be as easy as it sounds," said Ginger. "There'll be a lot to fix up first."

"Well, let's fix it up, then," said William.

Mr. Kellyngs paid his bill, took his leave of Mrs. Barnet and set off on the road towards the station, carrying his suit-case in one hand and the attaché-case containing his manuscript in the other. He walked slowly, enjoying the peace of the countryside. He had left himself ample time to catch the eleven-thirty, and there was no need to hurry. Turning round, he saw that three or four boys were walking just behind him, but three or four boys were generally walking just behind him or just in front of him or by his side. It had never occurred to Mr. Kellyngs to notice that it was the same three or four boys who accompanied him on each occasion. He merely thought that the village was over-populated with boys of that particular size. He realised that they were now walking abreast of him—two on one side and one on the other.

"Shall I carry your suit-case for you?" said one in a quavering high-pitched voice.

"No, thank you," said Mr. Kellyngs shortly.

"Shall I carry your 'taché case?" said another in a voice so sharply falsetto that it nearly made Mr. Kellyngs drop both cases into the road.

"No, thank you," said Mr. Kellyngs.

He didn't trust children and he didn't intend to let his attaché-case out of his hand till he had deposited it safely in his publisher's office.

"It wouldn't be any trouble," barked the third child. "We'd like to help you."

"No, thank you," said Mr. Kellyngs again. "I prefer to carry my own cases."

The children exchanged significant glances.

"Well, that jolly well *proves* it, Hector the Dare-Devil," said one.

"Yes, it jolly well does, Henrico the Terrible," said another.

"Well, now I must hurry, my little men," said Mr. Kellyngs in a tone of dismissal. "I'm catching the eleven-thirty and must get on to the station."

"Gosh!" said one of them. "Didn't you know about the strike?"

"What strike?" said Mr. Kellyngs.

"The railway strike."

"Good Heavens!" he said. "No one told me and I haven't opened my newspaper this morning. What a nuisance! Just today when it's most important that I should get to London." His irritation rose. "But surely I can't be the only passenger. Someone must be in charge of the arrangements."

The boy with the curious bleating voice spoke.

"The person in charge of *your* arrangements is over there in the old barn."

Mr. Kellyngs looked at the ramshackle building that could be seen at the end of the field that bordered the road. Relief and perplexity was visible in his face.

"How strange!" he said. "But I suppose they're chartering a coach and assembling the passengers there. Well, I mustn't waste any more time."

"We'll take you to it," said the boy who barked like a dog. "It's this way . . . over the stile."

The procession wended its way across the field.

Ginger and Douglas fell behind the other two.

76

"I've not had time to show you this before," whispered Ginger, bringing a cardboard box out of his pocket, "but it's something pretty deadly. The greengrocer's boy found it in a crate of bananas this mornin' and he swapped it with me for my ninepenny 'bus ticket." He opened the box a fraction of an inch, revealing a bloated-looking spider with a furry body, then quickly closed it again. "Its bite," he continued impressively, "is certain death. The boy said it was an' he ought to know."

"Gosh! " said Douglas.

"We'll only use it if we have to, of course," said Ginger, "but he's a jolly savage crim'nal. You can see that by lookin' at him. He's prob'ly got razor blades hid all over him. We'll only use the spider 'case he gets so savage it's a matter of life an' death."

"How will it know which to bite?" said Douglas nervously. "The spider, I mean."

"Dunno," said Ginger. "I never thought of that. Tell you what. If he starts gettin' savage, I'll slip it in the case where he's got his atom bomb papers an' then when he opens it he'll get the bite that's certain death. I don't *want* to do it, of course, 'cause it's a jolly serious thing givin' a person a bite that's certain death, even an atom bomb stealer. . . . Anyway, p'raps he won't get savage. P'raps he'll jus' think William's Stalin, same as we want him to, an' give him the papers an' go away."

Henry and Mr. Kellyngs were just entering the old barn.

William sat in an impressive attitude on a packing-case. His appearance had been copied faithfully (or rather as faithfully as possible) from the picture of Stalin in Henry's encyclopædia. He wore a golfing blouse of Robert's that engulfed his figure, Ethel's jockey cap, and a large straggling moustache that Robert had once worn

77

"Hail, Comrade!" said William

in some amateur theatricals and that fell off whenever he moved.

Mr. Kellyngs stood staring at him, open-mouthed with amazement. William rose to his feet with an air of dignity.

"Hail, Comrade! " he said, holding his moustache on with one hand and making a sweeping gesture with the other. "I'm Stalin come over to England to fetch thy papers about the atom bomb. I'm flyin' back to Russia 'ere nightfall an' I'll take them along with me. Thee will be well paid for thy trouble, but I haven't any change on me at present. I'll send thee a postal order from Russia when I get there. Hist! Not a word! Give me the papers and begone! "

The amazement on Mr. Kellyngs' face was swiftly changing to anger.

"What outrageous trick is this?" he fumed, putting his cases down on the ground.

"He's goin' to get savage," whispered Ginger. "He'll have his razor blades out in a second an' start wadin' in our blood. Come on! We'll have to do it."

Swiftly he opened his cardboard box and slipped its occupant into the attaché-case among Mr. Kellyngs' papers.

"What are you doing with my case, you little ruffian?" shouted Mr. Kellyngs. "How dare you tamper with it! "

"You'd better be careful," said William. "I've got a hundred Cossacks hid in the wood with deadly weapons an' if you don't give me those papers——"

Mr. Kellyngs had snatched up his case and opened it suspiciously in order to check its contents after Ginger's "tampering." Ginger had turned pale.

"Its bite is certain death," he said in a hollow voice.

The expression on Mr. Kellyngs' face had turned to one of delight.

"Nonsense! " he said. "It's a Brazilian spider that I've
79

been trying to find for years. This is wonderful! It——"

At that moment the vicar appeared in the doorway.

"I couldn't think what had happened to you, Kellyngs," he said. "I went to the station to see you off and was told that you'd been seen coming over the fields here. There's no time to lose if you're going to catch that train."

"But the railway strike?" said Mr. Kellyngs.

"There is no railway strike."

"But these boys told me there was. They brought me here to wait for some arrangements to be made about a coach or something."

The vicar turned his frowning gaze upon the Outlaws. He might have known it! They were at the bottom of every bit of trouble that ever happened in the village.

"There's no time to go into it now," he said. "But"— with menace in his voice—"I shall certainly see your fathers about this."

"No, please don't," said Mr. Kellyngs. He was beaming rapturously and replacing the spider in the cardboard box that he had taken from Ginger's inert hand. "They've found me the tarantula I've been wanting to get for years. I'll forgive them anything."

"Well, come along. Come along. Come along," said the vicar, and Mr. Kellyngs, snatching up his cases, set off at a run across the field.

The Outlaws stood at the door of the old barn, watching them.

"*Well!*" said William at last. "All that trouble for nothing!"

"He was a real naturalist, after all," said Henry despondently.

"I'm glad he didn't wade in our blood, anyway," said Douglas.

Then Ginger gave a sudden yell of excitement.

"*Look!*" he said. "Look! There it is!"

And there it was . . . a large cumbersome van with "Blessington's Amusements" painted on it, followed by the familiar train of caravans, ambling slowly along the country road.

"It's come! The fair's come!"

William stayed only to tear off his golf blouse and jockey cap, then the four of them, whooping with joy, ran down to join the crowd of excited small boys that formed the tail end of the procession.

Cats and White Elephants

"I MET Miss Milton in the village this morning," said Mrs. Brown. "She's having a White Elephant Sale, and she could talk of nothing else."

"*Not* another White Elephant Sale!" said Ethel.

"These White Elephant Sales of Miss Milton's are approaching a national calamity," said Mr. Brown.

"Oh, I don't know," said Robert. "I don't think she's had one for at least ten days."

The Browns were at lunch, interspersing desultory conversation about local affairs with comments on William's table manners—comments that were so usual a part of any conversation at meals that they came as naturally as the act of drawing breath.

"I wonder there's a White Elephant left in the place," said Ethel.

"Yes, the breed must be almost exterminated by now," agreed Mr. Brown.

D

"William, must you drink like that?" groaned Ethel.

"I only drink same as other people," said William with spirit. "I put water in my mouth an' swallow it. It's news to *me* there's any other way of drinkin'. If you'll kin'ly tell me any other way of drinkin'——"

"Be quiet, William," said Mr. Brown.

"The pièce de résistance of the last one," said Robert, "was a shoehorn of Victorian design priced at ten shillings. . . . William, I wish you'd keep your elbows to yourself."

William assumed a crippled attitude, elbows pressed into his sides, hands hanging helplessly, but, as no one took any notice of him, he abandoned it and proceeded with his lunch.

"The last one taught her a lesson," said Mrs. Brown, "because hardly anyone bought anything. She's not going to charge more than two-and-six for anything at this one. William, don't play with your food."

"I'm not axshully playin' with it," explained William. "I'm workin' out what'd happen if this carrot was a glacier an'——"

"Be quiet, William," said Mr. Brown.

"I shall have to send something, I suppose," said Mrs. Brown. "It isn't till the day after to-morrow, but Miss Milton always has everything ready at least two days beforehand. Don't slouch like that, William. You'll be growing up round-shouldered, if you aren't careful, and then what will you do?"

"I could be a jockey," said William, after giving the matter a moment's deep thought. "A jockey's got to be round-shouldered. I bet jockeys *practice* bein' round-shouldered an'——"

"Be quiet, William," said Mr. Brown.

The telephone bell rang, and Ethel went to answer it. She returned a few moments later, frowning thoughtfully.

"It was Peggy Barton," she said. "She wants me to go

over there this afternoon and help her with a hair perm. She can't put it off because she's going to a dance to-morrow night. And she helped me with mine last month."

"Well, you can go and help her, can't you, dear?" said Mrs. Brown.

"The nuisance of it is that I'm going to tea with Archie this afternoon."

"Archie! " said the Browns on varying notes of pity, incredulity and amusement.

"Didn't I tell you?" said Ethel, looking self-conscious. "It's his birthday, and he's been pestering me for months to go to tea with him on his birthday, and at last I said I would, simply because I couldn't keep on thinking out reasons why I couldn't."

"Well, you're a brave girl," said Robert. "I heard that the last person who went to tea with Archie got sand-wiches of floor polish and salad cream in their tea."

"Nonsense, Robert! " said Mrs. Brown.

"I once drank some paraffin, 'cause it was in a lemonade bottle," said William, "an' everything I ate for years afterwards tasted of it. I'd almost got to like it in the end, 'cause——"

"Be quiet, William," said Mr. Brown.

"But you could go to tea with Archie after you'd done Peggy's hair, couldn't you, dear?" said Mrs Brown.

"Yes, if I hadn't got to fetch the cat," said Ethel.

"The *cat*! " said the Browns with heightened emotion.

"I'm giving him a cat for his birthday present," said Ethel. "I had to give him something. He gave me that marvellous compact on my birthday, and he's overrun with mice, and he's been wanting a cat for ages. He says that one of his most beautiful childhood memories is a ginger cat on a black hearthrug, and when I saw a ginger cat at Emmett's yesterday I bought it on impulse. I re-gretted it as soon as I'd done it and it seemed so silly that I didn't tell you, but, anyway, I'd arranged to fetch it this afternoon and take it straight to Archie's and—well, if I go to do Peggy's perm, I don't see how I can."

A flicker of interest had come into William's eyes.

"I don't mind fetchin' the cat for you, Ethel," he said with rather overdone nonchalance. "I've got a bit of time to spare this afternoon, an' I'd like to do a little thing like that to help you."

Ethel gave him a meaning look. It meant quite a lot of things, but gratitude was not among them.

"I remember a certain other occasion when you offered to fetch a cat from Emmett's," she said coldly.

William assumed an expression of enquiring innocence.

"When was that, Ethel?" he said.

"You remember perfectly well," said Ethel shortly. "You were supposed to be bringing me a white cat from Mr. Romford as a birthday present, and—well, perhaps you remember what happened."

William tried to retain the expression of enquiring innocence, but without much success.

"Oh, that!" he said, as if dimly recalling something through the mists of time. "I do remember somethin' about it, but it was so long ago, I'd nearly forgot. It—it sort of got out, didn't it?"

"It sort of ended up as a ferret," said Ethel bitterly.

"Oh, well," said William, vaguely apologetic, "but I wouldn't let a cat out of a basket now, Ethel. I've got a bit more sense than that now."

"It's not noticeable," said Ethel.

"It will be in a basket, won't it, Ethel?" said Mrs. Brown.

"Oh, yes. Mr. Emmett's lending me a cat basket to carry it in."

"Well, dear, I really think you might let William do it. That is, if you really want to help Peggy with her perm."

"Of course I do. I shall want her to help me with mine again in a few months' time."

"The word 'permanent'," said Mr. Brown as he folded up his table napkin and rose from the table, "appears to be somewhat of an over-statement."

"Oh, it's permanent, all right," explained Ethel, "but it only lasts a few months."

As the door closed on Mr. Brown and Robert, Ethel turned a thoughtful look on William.

"If I could be sure . . ." she said in a tone of one who weakens against her better judgment.

William hastened to pursue his advantage.

"You needn't worry about it, Ethel," he said. "Gosh! I can do a little thing like fetchin' a cat. Think of the people that fetch bears an' lions an' tigers an' hippopotamuses to circuses an' zoos an' things, an' I bet I could do it as well as they do, so it'd be a funny thing if I couldn't fetch a cat."

The logic of this obviously failed to impress Ethel, but there was still weakening in her glance.

"I think I should let him try if I were you, Ethel," said Mrs. Brown. "He's done one or two errands for me very nicely lately."

"Yes," said Ethel, "especially the time when he dropped that bag of flour in the road and scooped half the road back into it."

"Yes, but listen," said William earnestly. "Flour's different from a cat. An', anyway, I bet you'd never have known about that bit of earth that got in with it if it hadn't been a diff'rent colour. I bet it'd've *tasted* all right. . . . An', anyway, this cat won't be in a paper bag, an' baskets don't bust open all by themselves without you doin' anythin' to them same as paper bags do. Well," with a short ironic laugh, "it's news to *me* if they do."

"William, do stop using that idiotic expression," said Mrs. Brown.

"If there was any other way . . ." said Ethel.

"I can fetch it, then, can I, Ethel?" said William.

"I suppose so," said Ethel with a shrug of resignation.

"Gosh! *Thanks!*" said William. "Well," importantly, "I'd better get started. Can't keep that ole cat waitin'."

"Now don't dash off like that, William," said Mrs. Brown. "Listen carefully and be quite sure what you have to do. You must fetch the cat from Emmett's, take it straight to Archie's and tell him that Ethel will be with him for tea but may be a few minutes late. Now is that clear?"

"Yes," said William, adding tentatively, "I wouldn't mind goin' to tea with Archie, too. I like playin' in his rock'ry pond and somethin' int'restin' gen'rally happens when I'm there. The last time I went I opened a tin of sardines for him with the bread knife 'cause he'd lost his tin-opener an' I cut my finger an' he put cough mixture on it 'cause he thought it was iodine an' he lent me his handkerchief for a bandage."

"Yes, that reminds me," said Mrs. Brown. "I washed it and you can take it back to-day."

"He said I could keep it," said William.

"Of course you mustn't keep it, dear. It's in the hat-stand drawer all ready to go back."

"I'll write a card for you to take," said Ethel. "The creature's called Horace. He might as well know its name so that he can start making friends with it."

A few moments later, William issued jauntily from the front door, Archie's handkerchief, neatly folded, in one pocket and Ethel's card in the other.

"Jumble!" he called.

After the fifth summons, Jumble came leaping through the hedge of the next-door garden, jumping up at William

in a manner that suggested joyful reunion after long
and painful separation.

"Good ole Jumble!" said William and swaggered on
down the road. His sense of importance rose at every
step. He wasn't a boy going to fetch a cat for his sister.
He was a famous circus-owner going to collect a few
more lions and tigers for his circus. He had already
collected wild animals from every part of the globe. His
circus was world-famous. He stood in the ring cracking
his whip. Lions, tigers, hyenas, bears circled round him.

"Down, there! Down! he shouted, then, "Good ole
boy!" to a lion who had just walked the tight-rope to
thunderous applause. "You next!" to a panther who had
just walked into the ring. "Get back there!" he called
to an attendant who had rashly advanced to the tight-
rope. "He'll mangle anyone but me. I'm the only one he
doesn't mangle. Go on, ole chap," said William en-
couragingly. "Get up an' walk along the rope." Obediently
the panther got up and walked along the rope. It was the
end of the performance. Deafening applause arose.
William, surrounded by his wild beasts, stood bowing
his acknowledgments, one hand on the lion's head, the
other on the panther's.

"Ladies an' gentlemen——" he began and almost
collided with Ginger, Henry and Douglas who were just
turning the bend of the road.

"Hello," said Ginger. "Where are you goin'? We were
just coming to fetch you."

William returned abruptly to earth.

"I'm fetchin' a cat," he said.

"Why?" said Ginger.

"Where from?" said Douglas.

"Where to?" said Henry.

Their interest was flattering, and the facts of the case
were suddenly too tame to suit William's exalted mood.

"It's a specially savage cat," he said airily, "an' Ethel wanted me to fetch it 'cause she knows I'm good with wild animals. I didn't want to fetch it, 'cause I'm busy this afternoon, but she begged an' begged me to, 'cause she knew I'm the only one that wild animals don't mangle. Well," he gave a short laugh as his day-dream suddenly became real again, "cats are nothin' to me. Cats are jus' *nothin'* to me."

The Outlaws were sufficiently accustomed to William to discount something of his grandiloquence. Still—it was probably true that he was going to fetch a cat, and the situation might turn out to be interesting.

"We'll come along with you," said Ginger.

"All right," agreed William, who always liked to have witnesses of his more important rôles.

"Where are you fetching it from?" said Douglas.

"Emmett's," said William. He thought of Mr. Emmett's animal shop. It had always seemed to him a place as near paradise as earth could offer, but, with the spell of his day-dream still upon him, it shrank to pigmy proportions, became small and dull and devoid of glamour. "I bet ole Emmett'll be glad to have a chat with me. I bet lions an' tigers don't often come his way." He gave his short ironic laugh. "Well, it's news to *me* if lions an' tigers come ole Emmett's way."

"He had a dancing mouse when I was there once," said Ginger.

"Gosh! Did he really?" said William eagerly, forgetting his rôle. "I wish I'd seen it."

Discussing the subject of dancing mice and the possibility of evolving a strain of dancing hens from Ginger's mother's Buff Orpington, they made their way over the fields and down by the short cut to Hadley. Jumble frisked about them, plunging into rabbit holes, worrying twigs, disappearing into ditches after imaginary water-rats.

Occasionally William would call, in a curt authoritative manner, "Hi, Jumble! To heel! "—a phrase which Jumble always interpreted as an invitation to explore the distant horizon.

"He's jolly intelligent," William would say in explanation of this, for Jumble was, in any and every circumstance, a dog without a flaw in William's eyes. "He mus' have seen somethin' int'restin' over there an' thought I was tellin' him to go after it."

The conversation then turned to the ginger cat.

"What colour *is* a ginger cat?" said Douglas.

"Same colour as Ginger's hair," said Henry.

While Ginger was wondering whether or not to resent this is an insult, William said:

"Well, I don't think it is same as Ginger's hair. I think it's yellow."

"It isn't. Ginger means brown."

"It doesn't. It means red."

"It doesn't. It means yellow."

"D'you think I don't know what ginger means? Ginger's hair's brown, isn't it?"

"No, it's red."

"You shut up about my hair," burst out Ginger, whose resentment had been silently gathering force during the conversation. "If you think you can go on an' on about a person's hair an'——"

A diversion was created by Jumble, who, becoming exasperated by his failure to unearth any rabbits, had started chasing a couple of cows across the field.

"It's jolly clever of him," said William. "He's doin' it same as those tornados do in It'ly."

"Toreadors," said Henry, "an' Spain."

"Well, there's not much diff'rence between It'ly an' Spain," said William, aggressively. "They're spelt a bit diff'rent, that's all. I've always thought I'd like to be one

89

of those tor—bull-fighters myself. I tried once with that antelope's head in the hall, but it wasn't any good, 'cause the hat-stand fell down. Anyway, I don't see why there shouldn't be tornado dogs same as tornado men, an' I don't see why Jumble shouldn't be one."

Jumble, however, evidently deciding against this career, abandoned his cows and returned to William; and the four Outlaws, considerably hampered by Jumble, climbed the stile that led to the main Hadley road.

Emmett's, the animal shop, was a fascinating medley of tortoises, puppies, kittens, rabbits, canaries, guinea-pigs, mice, rats and gold-fish. The Outlaws stood gazing around them, spell-bound. No spell, however, bound Jumble, and he leapt with shrill barks of excitement at the nearest rabbit hutch, precipitating it on to the floor.

Mr. Emmett came forward from behind the counter.

"No dogs allowed in here unless on a lead," he said sternly, pointing to a notice on the wall.

"I'll hold him," said William, grabbing Jumble by the collar, while Mr. Emmett restored the rabbit hutch to its original position. "He's had leads but he eats 'em."

"What can I do for you?" said Mr. Emmett impatiently. "Leave those tortoises alone, my boy."

Ginger transferred his attention to the guinea-pigs, while Henry and Douglas tried to fraternise with a couple of white rats.

"I've come for Ethel's cat," said William, restraining Jumble with difficulty, for Jumble had just caught sight of a Siamese cat and was anxious to pursue the acquaintance.

"Oh, yes . . . Miss Brown's ginger. He's all ready . . . Don't touch those rats, please, boys, and put that cage of mice down. . . . I'll just get him."

With a harassed glance at his customers, Mr. Emmett turned to go into the back regions of his shop. Jumble, having worked the Siamese into a frenzy of rage, now started trying to make friends with a tortoise, waving his tail ingratiatingly and planting his front paws ready for a romp.

Mr. Emmett hurried back into the shop, carrying a square basket with a handle.

"Here he is," he said. "He's had a good feed of fish and milk, so he won't need feeding again to-day. Carry him carefully. Put that bird cage down, my boy."

"What's this?" said Ginger, who had gone into the darkest corner of the shop and was examining a small cage.

"That, my boy," said Mr. Emmett "is a jerboa. A species of rodent."

"What's a rodent?" said Douglas.

"An animal that gnaws," said Mr. Emmett shortly. "Now off you go, boys! Where's that dog?"

Interest in the jerboa had made William let go his hold on Jumble's collar, and at first it seemed that Jumble had disappeared. After a brief search, however, he was discovered behind the counter, hard at work on an open sack of dog biscuits.

Mr. Emmett heaved a sigh of relief when finally the four boys trooped out of the shop with Jumble and the cat basket. Jumble pranced on ahead, intent only, as it seemed, on getting under the feet of the passers-by and entangling himself with prams and scooters.

"I'll carry the basket if you like, William," said Ginger wistfully.

"No, you won't," said William. "I'll carry it."

"It's jolly quiet."

"P'raps it's asleep."

"I liked that gnawbill," said William.

"Jerboa," said Henry. "A rodent that gnaws."

"Well, I said that, didn't I?" said William.

91

"Listen!" said Ginger excitedly.

They listened. A hissing scratching sound was coming from inside the basket.

"Gosh! It's woke up all right," said William.

"I should think so!" said Douglas. "Anyone'd wake up bein' swung about like you've been doin'."

"Well, a cat oughtn't to mind a bit of swingin'," said William, adding, with a modest air of knowledge, "They swing cats to see if there's room enough in places."

"Let's have a look at it," said Henry. "Through the chinks, I mean. We're jolly well not goin' to open it."

They stood and examined the basket, pressing their eyes to the chinks.

"You can't see much."

"Yes, look! I can see a bit of fur. It's brown."

"An' I can see a bit an it's yellow."

Jumble took a flying leap in hot pursuit of the cat

"I told you it was yellow."

"I told you it was brown."

"Well, I can see a bit an' it's red."

"Pity we can only see it in bits," said Ginger.

There was a silence in which the same thought gradually took shape in all their minds.

"Look!" said William, putting the thought into words. "We won't open it. Not axshully *open* it. Not *right* open. That other ole cat got away 'cause I axshully opened it. But, if we jus' undid the catch an' jus' peeped inside we could have a look at it. I only mean a teeny bit of an inch. That couldn't do any harm. Well, a cat couldn't get out of a teeny bit of an inch, could it? Stands to reason it couldn't. Not a whole cat. There wouldn't be *room* for it to get out of a teeny bit of an inch."

"We oughtn't to," said Douglas. "I bet it'll get us in a muddle."

"How could it?" said William, whose last scruple

93

had now disappeared. "Jus' kin'ly tell me how it could." He repeated his short ironic laugh. "Well, it's news to *me* that a whole cat can get out of a teeny bit of an inch. 'Tisn't as if it was a little thing like a gerbeak."

"Jerboa," said Henry. "A rodent that gnaws."

"Well, that's what I keep sayin', isn't it?" said William irritably. "You mus' be deaf . . . Look. I'll open it jus' a teeny bit of an inch; then we can make sure. . . ."

They crowded round him. He undid the catch and opened the basket a few inches. Then, before anyone realised what was happening, Jumble had taken a flying leap, scattered both Outlaws and basket and was vanishing in the distance in hot pursuit of a ginger cat.

"Gosh!" gasped William. "Come on! Let's catch him! Quick!"

They tore over the brow of the hill and down to the stile on the other side. Neither Jumble nor the ginger cat was anywhere to be seen.

"They mus' have gone into the woods," said William. "Come on."

"I *told* you we'd get into a muddle," said Douglas.

"P'raps it's the darkest hour before the dawn," said Ginger, who had studied a book of proverbs and proverbial sayings on the railway bookstall the last time he had gone to London with his mother.

"Oh, shut up an' come on," said William.

A search of the wood proved fruitless. There was no trace of Jumble or the ginger cat.

"We'll get in an awful row," said Douglas.

"An' it's all that ole Jumble's fault," said Ginger.

"It isn't," said William indignantly. "Jumble's a jolly intelligent dog. He knew if he was goin' to be a tornado dog, he'd got to start on somethin' small before he could start on bulls, an' it was jolly clever of him to think of startin' on cats."

94

"Well, we've not got a present for Archie," said Ginger, "an' that's goin' to be jolly serious, 'cause Ethel's goin' there to tea, an' time an' tide wait for no man."

"Oh, shut up sayin' things like that," snapped William. "Tell you what! S'pose we go back to Emmett's an' see if he'll let us have that gerrybilt mouse——"

"Jerboa," said Henry. "A rodent that gnaws."

"I keep on an' on sayin' that," said William. "You don't understand English. That's what's wrong with you."

"There's not time to go back to Hadley," said Douglas. "We'd better have another try at findin' it."

"All right," said William. "Let's split up. Ginger an' me'll go along this way an' you an' Henry go along that way an'"—his optimism returning—"I bet we find it soon now."

But his optimism ebbed, as a search of the village revealed no signs of the missing pair.

"Now listen," said William at last. "I don't want Archie to think that Ethel's not got him a present when she goes there to tea. It might put him in a bad temper so's he wouldn't let us play in his rock'ry pond. I think we ought to get him somethin' jus' to be goin' on with, jus' till we find that cat."

"Well, it's early closin' day in the village," said Ginger, "so we can't buy anything."

A thoughtful look was coming over William's face.

"N-no," he said, "but I remember my mother was sayin' something about a White Elephant Sale at Miss Milton's. That's a sort of shop. We might find a nice present for him there."

"That's not till the day after to-morrow. My mother was talking about it, too."

"No, but my mother said she gets it ready two days beforehand. It'll probably be ready now. An' there's goin'

95

to be nothin' over half a crown. How much money have you got?"

"I've got three halfpence in coppers," said Ginger. "How much have you got?"

"I've got some bits of a two-shilling piece," said William. "It was a bad one that Robert had an' he broke it an' gave me the bits."

"We could stick 'em together," suggested Ginger.

"I tried doin' that," said William, "an' it wasn't any good. I got glue all over my fingers so I had to help with my teeth an' I swallowed one of the bits by mistake, so it isn't any good now. Not as a two-shilling piece. I don't s'pose it's worth more than twopence halfpenny now, with one of the bits gone." Then a light broke out over his sombre countenance. "*Tell* you what! I've got an idea."

"What?" said Ginger.

"There's that hanky of Archie's. He said I could keep it—he *gave* it me—an' it'd make a jolly good White Elephant. I bet it cost more than half a crown. It's a good one. It's got sewing round the edge with little holes in. We'll take it to this Sale of Miss Milton's an' ask her to change it for somethin' for Archie's birthday present. Jus' till we find the cat. We can change it back after that."

"All right," said Ginger with a puzzled frown. The whole situation was getting a bit beyond him.

"Well, come on," said William briskly. "We've got a lot to get through an' we mustn' waste any more time."

Together they set off for Miss Milton's house with an alacrity that flagged somewhat as they drew near the gate. There they stood, looking at the house in secret apprehension. Miss Milton was a redoubtable lady, and their general rule was to confine their dealings with her to a minimum.

"Well, come on," said William at last. "We'll jus' say we've come to exchange a White Elephant for another White Elephant. It mus' be quite an ordin'ry thing to do. I say! "—his spirits rising—"she might have a ginger cat for a White Elephant. It'd be jolly lucky if she did."

"I bet she wouldn't have," said Ginger.

"Well, I only said she *might*. She might have one of those geranium mice too. Those gnawin' ones. I'd sooner have one of those than a cat any day. . . . Well, I s'pose I'd better ring her bell. The las' time I knocked her knocker she said I'd never to knock it again 'cause it gave her a headache for a week."

He pressed his finger on the bell and waited. Nothing happened. He pressed the bell again. Still nothing happened.

"The door's not quite shut," said Ginger.

"Well, let's go in, then," said William. "I bet it's all right. A White Elephant Sale's the same as a shop an' you go into shops without knockin' at the door or ringin' at the bell."

He pushed open the door and entered the hall. Ginger followed a little nervously. The hall was empty. William hesitated a moment, then opened the door of the sitting-room and went in, followed by Ginger.

"Well, there's nothin' here," said Ginger, looking round.

But William had espied Miss Milton's "silver table" that stood between the two windows. On it were several snuff-boxes, a Queen Anne pepper-pot, a silver vase, the silver trowel that had been presented to Miss Milton's grandfather on the occasion of the laying of the foundation stone of the Working Men's Club, a silver thimble that had belonged to Miss Milton's mother and a silver-framed photograph of Miss Milton at the age of eighteen, wearing a simpering smile and a gauze scarf.

97

E

"Look! This mus' be it," said William, pointing to the table. "It's a sort of stall."

"But they're all silver things," said Ginger.

"Well, that's all right," said William. "Robert was talkin' about a silver shoehorn at her las' White Elephant Sale, so I 'spect she does have silver things."

"Well, there's nothin' here Archie'd want," said Ginger. "Vases an' awful photographs."

"Yes, look!" said William excitedly. "There's a pepper-pot. I heard him say las' week he wanted a pepper-pot. It's a silly sort of shape but it'll be all right for pepper."

"What're you goin' to do about the handkerchief?" said Ginger.

"We'll jus' leave it here," said William carelessly, "same as people do pennies for newspapers. I 'spect that's what she means people to do—jus' come in an' leave somethin' an' take somethin' else 'stead of it."

He burrowed in his pocket, scattering its contents round his feet, till he found the handkerchief, now firmly attached to a damp and fluffy humbug.

"I'll put it on the table with the other things," he said indistinctly, as he bit the humbug off and began to crunch it.

He put the handkerchief on the table, picked up the penknife, bits of string, lumps of putty, acorns, pencil, matchbox and marbles which, together with a toy pistol, Ethel's note and some fragments of dog biscuit, formed the contents of his pocket, took up the pepper-pot, rammed the whole collection unceremoniously back into his pockets, and prepared to depart.

"We'll go'n' give it to Archie," he said, "an' then we'll have another look for that cat an' if we find the cat we'll take the pepper-pot back to the White Elephant Sale an' get the handkerchief back."

" 'S a bit complicated," said Ginger perplexedly.

"No, it isn't," said William. "It's one of the simplest muddles I've ever been in. I keep on 'splainin' that I don't want Archie to think Ethel's not given him a present, 'cause it might hurt his feelings an' then he might stop lettin' us play in his rock'ry pond. Oh, come on an' stop wastin' time arguin'."

The two went out of the house and down the road to Archie's cottage. Archie could be seen at the bottom of his back garden. He had suddenly realised that he had no flowers in the sitting-room, where he hoped to entertain Ethel, so he had taken a vase down to the bed where a few weary nasturtiums struggled for existence in a colony of nettles. It never occurred to Archie to take the flowers to the vase. He took the vase to the flowers. He had that sort of mentality.

"We won't waste time goin' down there to him," said William. "We've got to find that cat. Come on. Let's put the pepper-pot on the table with Ethel's card an' then go back to that cat-hunt."

He opened the door and went into the sitting-room. Almost immediately Henry and Douglas arrived. They carried a gold-fish in a bowl.

"Look!" panted Douglas. "We couldn' find that cat, so we thought we'd get somethin' else, so we got this."

"Our gardener's wife gave it us," said Henry. "She won a flower vase at hoop-la at the fair, an' she's got that on the table in her front room now, so she doesn't need the gold-fish. She said its face was gettin' on her nerves, anyway."

"Yes, but we've got a pepper-pot," said William. "We don't want a pepper-pot *an'* a gold-fish."

"A gold-fish is better," said Douglas, " 'cause, after all, a gold-fish *is* an animal. I mean, it's more like a cat than a pepper-pot is. If we can't find the cat, I think a

99

gold-fish is nex' best. It's better than a pepper-pot, anyway."

"Y-yes," agreed William reluctantly, "but he hasn't
got a pepper-pot."

"Well, he hasn't got a gold-fish," said Henry.

"We'll have to take the pepper-pot back, then," said
Ginger.

"No, we've not time to do that now," said William.
"We'll take it back when we've found the cat." His eye
roved round the room. "We'll leave it here. Look! We'll
put it on the mantelpiece jus' behind that calendar, then,
when we've got the cat, we can take it back to Miss
Milton. Where's that card Ethel wrote?" He burrowed
again in his pocket and finally drew out the card, now
grubby and crumpled, and propped it up against the
gold-fish bowl on the table. They examined it with interest. It read: "This is Horace, with my love and best
wishes for your birthday. Ethel."

"I bet he'd sooner have it than a cat," said Douglas.
"It's not got claws."

"Well, we've got to find the cat," said William, "an' I
bet it won't take us long now."

"There's many a slip," said Ginger darkly, " 'twixt
cup and lip."

"Quick! " said William, looking out of the window,
"Archie's comin' back. We don't want him to find us
here 'cause we don't want to waste a lot of time 'splainin'
to him. Come on! "

The four went hurriedly out of the front door and
down to the gate.

"Let's sep'rate again," said William. "I bet we find
it in no time now."

Henry and Douglas set off across the fields, and Ginger
and William went towards the village. Passing Miss
Milton's cottage, they looked with interest through the
100

window into the room where Miss Milton could be seen standing in earnest contemplation of her "silver table."

"I bet she's feelin' jolly pleased with that handkerchief," said William complacently.

Miss Milton stood gazing with horror and indignation at the handkerchief she held in her hand. It had slipped on to the floor from the table where William had put it, and she had found it only after discovering the loss of the pepper-pot. Her Queen Anne silver pepper-pot . . . one of her greatest treasures . . . a family heirloom.

It had obviously been stolen while she was in the garage, setting out the things for her White Elephant stall on the trestle table that she kept there for that purpose. It happened that the bell was out of order, but in any case the thief would hardly have advertised his presence by ringing the bell. He had crept quietly in, stolen the pepper-pot and, had it not been that he had inadvertently dropped his handkerchief, would never have been detected. But the thief had dropped his handkerchief, and the handkerchief was Archie Mannister's. The name tab T. A. Mannister left no room for doubt.

Miss Milton was shocked but not incredulous. Archie Mannister was an artist and Miss Milton had always believed that artists were capable of anything. Archie was of good family, but the newspapers were full of stories of young men of good family who entangled themselves in crime and got themselves into police courts and prisons. The very fact that Archie was so unlike a criminal was, in Miss Milton's eyes, further proof that he was one.

Her tight prim mouth grew tighter and primmer as she reviewed the situation. Her duty was plain. She would finish arranging the things for her White Elephant Sale (Miss Milton had made it a rule from childhood to finish whatever she was doing before she started anything else), then she would go to Archie's cottage and tax him with his crime. After that she would report the matter to the police.

Archie, who was not at his best as a housekeeper, had had a difficult afternoon. The flues had gone wrong; the butter, which he had taken frozen solid from the refrigerator, and put on a saucer over the boiling kettle to melt, had slid gracefully from its saucer into the boiling kettle; the scones that he was toasting at the grill had chosen the moment when he was coping with the butter to go up in flames; the sugar that he had scattered lavishly over the sandwich cake had turned out to be salt; and he couldn't find the jam . . . but the smile with which he greeted Ethel on her arrival was one of undiluted bliss. For months he had been trying to persuade Ethel to come to tea with him and now she had come. . . .

"Do come in," he stammered ecstatically. "Do come in, Ethel. This is wonderful."

"Many happy returns of the day, Archie," said Ethel kindly.

In the intervals of her more exciting love affairs, Ethel was always ready to be kind to Archie.

They entered the sitting-room. Archie drew up an armchair and fussed about with footstools and cushions. Ethel looked around.

"Did William bring Horace?" she said.

"Oh, yes," said Archie. "I heard his voice when I was in the garden and when I came in I found that he'd left Horace with your beautiful note. It was a wonderful thought, Ethel. Thank you so much."

"Well, he should be company in the long winter evenings," said Ethel, "and they're not much trouble to feed. Just fish, and a little milk when you can spare it."

Archie looked startled.

"Oh . . . I shouldn't have thought of that."

"What would you have fed him on?"

"Well—er—ants' eggs, I think."

"Ants' eggs!" Ethel laughed. "How ridiculous! Please don't try feeding him on those. . . . He's very handsome, isn't he?"

"Er—yes," agreed Archie.

"He'll look rather sweet on your black hearthrug, won't he?"

Again Archie looked startled.

"I—I hadn't thought of putting him there," he said.

Ethel smiled.

"I expect he'll go there by himself," she said. Archie blinked. "Anyway, I hope he'll keep your mice down. Does he look as if he would?"

Archie's bewilderment was increasing.

"N-n-no," he stammered. "Actually he d-d-doesn't."

"I expect he will," said Ethel carelessly. She looked round the room. "Where is he now, by the way?"

"I've put him in the pond," said Archie. He beamed happily as he spoke. He couldn't have made a mistake there, anyway.

Ethel stared at him blankly.

"You've—*what*?" she said.

The frigidity of her voice told him that he *had* made a mistake, but he couldn't think how.

"P-put him in the p-pond," he stammered.

"And may I ask why?" said Ethel through tight lips.

"I thought it the best place for him," explained Archie simply.

And then came the rat-tat-tat at the door that heralded the arrival of Miss Milton. Archie rose with a sigh and admitted her. She stood in the doorway of the sitting-room, her eyes fixed accusingly on Archie.

"My errand, Archibald," she said, "is not a pleasant one."

Archie gaped at her.

"I have proof, Archibald," continued Miss Milton, "definite proof, that you have stolen my Queen Anne silver pepper-pot."

Archie gaped at her, but no sound came from his lips. Ethel was the first to recover from her stupor.

"What do you mean, Miss Milton?" she said.

"I'm sorry if this is a shock to you, Ethel," said Miss Milton kindly. "You naturally wouldn't expect to discover that Archie was a thief."

"There's not much I wouldn't expect to discover about Archie," said Ethel bitterly, "considering that he's just told me he's drowned my cat."

At that Archie found his voice—a high-pitched bleating voice of horror.

"Drowned your—— I don't know what you're talking about, Ethel. I've never touched your cat. I didn't even know you had one."

"*What?*" said Ethel, indignantly. "Do you mean to say that——"

"To return to the pepper-pot," interrupted Miss Milton. "I repeat that I have definite proof that you have stolen it."

"I've never even seen it," cried Archie wildly. "I think everyone's gone mad."

Miss Milton's gaze had wandered to the chimney-piece, and suddenly her eyes seemed to start from her head. She reached a hand up and removed the calendar.

"Archibald! " she said pointing to the pepper-pot, "can you *still* deny that you stole it?"

"*Yes!*" whinnied Archie. "Yes, I can . . . I do . . . I——"

There was the sound of voices and the four Outlaws were seen walking up the path to the front door carrying a cat basket. They clattered noisily into the studio, and William put the cat basket down on the table, then a confused babel of voices arose as they all began to explain at once.

"Well, it got away——"

"So we took the pepper-pot——"

"Then we got the gold-fish."

" 'Cause she'd got a hoop-la vase——"

"An' anyway, its face was on her nerves——"

"An' then we found the cat in the butchers——"

"But we've not found Jumble yet——"

"So we've got to go out an' look for him now——"

"Well, now we've got the cat an' you've got the pepper-pot," said William, turning to Miss Milton, "can we kin'ly have our handkerchief back?"

Miss Milton, who was past the power of speech, merely looked at him, breathing hard.

Ethel had taken Horace from his basket. He sat down on the hearthrug and began to purr complacently.

"Sorry there's been a bit of a mess-up," continued William, "but we took a lot of trouble an'——"

"An' all's well that ends well," said Ginger.

But all hadn't ended yet. At that moment a brown whirlwind flung itself through the open french window and immediately the room was a bedlam of growling, spitting, hissing, barking. Horace leapt on to the table and knocked over the tea-pot. Jumble leapt after him and scattered the sugar basin. Horace dragged the table-cloth from the table, tore Miss Milton's stockings, scratched Archie's face as he bent down to pick up the china, then streaked off through the open window, followed by Jumble.

"Come on!" shouted William exultantly. "Let's go after 'em."

"No, William," said Ethel, intercepting him and

closing the french window. "Now will you please explain what's happened?"

The Outlaws walked slowly and disconsolately down the road. Jumble followed at their heels as decorously as if he had never chased a cat or wrecked a tea-table in his life.

"Well, she told me to 'splain an' I 'splained," said William dejectedly, "but she jus' didn't seem to understand. Girls never do. An' she's goin' to tell my father about it, an' I bet she makes it all sound quite diff'rent from what it really was an' I bet he won't listen to a word I say."

The other Outlaws made grunting sounds of agreement.

"It never rains," commented Ginger, "but it pours."

"Oh, shut up!" said William. "Cats an' White Elephants! There's no sense in 'em. If I was king of a country, I wouldn't have cats or White Elephants in it at all. I'd stop 'em by lor. I'd only have"—he looked down fondly at Jumble. Jumble was the cause of all the trouble, but, in William's eyes, he was still a dog without a flaw— "I'd only have dogs an'—an' "—the memory of the little bright-eyed creature was vivid in his mind, but the elusive word still eluded him—"an'—an' those little jergnawrers." He threw a defiant glance at Henry as he spoke and added, without waiting to be corrected, "Well, that's what I *said*, isn't it?"

106

The Pennyman's Hand on the Torch

THE Outlaws always kept a watchful eye upon the Hall and made the most of its frequent periods of emptiness. They had made an extensive study of the habits of caretakers, knew their (frequent) hours of repose and played undisturbed in the garden and sometimes even in the house itself.

But the arrival of new tenants interested them, too, because new tenants, though of course they might prove uninteresting, might also give to life that added zest that the Outlaws always liked life to have.

So when they heard that the Hall was let again, their disappointment at being deprived of their unofficial playground was tempered by excitement at the prospect of new neighbours.

They ascertained the time of their arrival in order to be the first to see the new-comers. The Outlaws generally did this when new people were coming to the village. One glance sufficed to tell the Outlaws whether the new-comer was capable of adding any sort of zest to life.

On this occasion the train was rather late and the Outlaws, clustered together on a stile on the road that led from the station to the Hall, grew restive. The Outlaws did not like wasting their time.

"I vote we go away," said Ginger, "we don't want to stay here *all* day, an' it's nearly ten minutes after the time now. We'll never get any decent game if we stay here *all* day."

"You can't call ten minutes all day," challenged William pugnaciously.

"Yes, you can," said Ginger, taking up the challenge with enthusiasm, for the ten minutes' inactivity was telling on his nerves. "*Course* you can. Ten minutes *an*' ten minutes *an*' ten minutes an' it's soon all day. We've had one ten minutes an' soon it'll be another, an' so on, an' that's all day if it goes on long enough, isn't it?"

"Well, you can't say it's all day after only *one* ten minutes," returned William, as pleased as Ginger at finding something to argue about. "It's a *lie* callin' *one* ten minutes a whole day. *Anyone* 'd say it was a lie. I bet if you asked *anyone* they'd say it was a lie, callin' one ten minutes a whole day."

Ginger was just going to make a spirited reply when Douglas said, "Here they are," and the station cab trotted slowly into view.

They fell silent and craned forward to look. The cabman, who owed William several, managed to give him one neat flick as he flourished his whip carelessly in passing. William tried to catch hold of the end, failed, and overbalanced into the field behind. He resumed his seat, rubbing the side of his face where the whip had caught it. The incident had stimulated him and turned his mind to pleasant thoughts of vengeance. There were certain perpetual feuds without which William would have found life almost unsupportable, and one of them was the feud with the village cabman. It came next in excitement and general indispensability to the feud with Farmer Jenks.

But the horse was an ancient horse whom nothing could ever induce to move at more than a walking pace, and so, even with this little interlude, William had plenty of time to inspect the occupants of the cab. There were two—a man and a woman, both very tall, very pale and very thin. Both wore pince-nez and hand-woven tweeds.

The Outlaws gazed at them in silence till they had disappeared from view. Then Ginger said in a resigned tone of voice:

"Well, *they* don't look very int'restin'."

William, however, was not so sure. "You never know," he said, with an air of deep wisdom, "they *might* be. Anyway, I bet it's worth goin' to see 'em to-night."

The Outlaws generally followed up an acquaintance-ship begun in this way by paying an unofficial visit to the new-comer's house after dusk in order to study the household at closer quarters. People seldom drew blinds or curtains, and even if they did there was generally an aperture through which they could be studied.

"Might as well go an' *see*, anyway," repeated William. "We needn't stay if they keep on bein' dull. But you never know. People that look dull often turn out to be excitin'. An' sometimes the other way round."

They waited concealed in the ditch, as was their custom, for the return of the now empty cab, and as soon as it had safely passed them emerged to hang on behind till the cabman saw them and zestfully removed them with his whip.

Then, stimulated by the little diversion, they returned to the game of Red Indians that they had abandoned in order to perform their unofficial welcome of the new-comers.

Dusk found them creeping in single file through the grounds of the Hall on their way to the house where the new-comers should be spending their first evening in their new home.

A bright light shone from the uncurtained drawing-room window, and this the Outlaws cautiously approached. There was a convenient bush by it that would have screened them from view had it been daylight.

They crouched behind it and gazed into the room. And in the room was a marvellous sight. The tall thin lady and the tall thin gentleman had discarded their hand-woven tweeds and were dressed in flowing classical robes with fillets about their heads. The lady was working at a loom on one side of the fire and on the other the gentleman was playing unmelodiously but evidently to his own entire satisfaction upon a flute. The Outlaws stood and watched the scene spellbound. Then the spell was broken by a housemaid who opened the door and spoke. The window was open and the Outlaws could hear the conversation.

"Please, 'm, the butcher's come to see if there are any orders."

The effect of this remark was instantaneous and terrifying. The woman went pale and the man dropped his flute and both assumed an expression of almost unendurable suffering. For a minute they were silent, and it was clear that they were silent because their mental anguish was too intense for speech. Finally the woman spoke in a faint voice.

"Send him away," she said. "Send him right away. Tell him never to come back again. And—and Mary——" The maid who was preparing to go, turned back. "Never . . . *never* mention the word to us again."

"What word, 'm?" asked Mary innocently.

"The word, the word you said," said the lady.

The housemaid bridled indignantly.

"No langwidge what nobody mightn't hear has never passed my lips," she said pugnaciously, "not never in all me life."

"The word your mistress meant," said the man in a low pained voice, "was the—the name of the man who spills the blood of our little brothers and sisters."

"*Lor!*" said the maid, her eyes and mouth opening
110

to their fullest extent, "*Lor!* spills the b——. You've bin 'avin' nightmares, 'm. The police 'd get 'im quick if anyone went about doin' anythin' like that."

"No, no," said the man impatiently, "by brothers and sisters your mistress means our little *four-footed* brothers and sisters."

"Oh, *them*," said the maid. "Pigs and such-like. The butcher you mean, 'm, then?"

Again the lady and her husband blanched and exhibited signs of acute suffering.

"Don't. Please don't Never mention the word again. Tell him never to come near us again."

"You don't want no meat then?" inquired the maid innocently.

The word meat seemed to have as devastating an effect as the word butcher.

"Never!" moaned the lady, averting her head, making a gesture with her hand as if waving something aside. "We shall live on vegetables and on vegetables only. And we grow them ourselves. I meant to tell you earlier, but have been too busy. We live the life that nature meant us to live. And macaroni. Macaroni that we make with our own hands and spread out to dry in the sun." The maid departed, and the lady and gentleman continued their weaving and flute playing. Suddenly the gentleman put down his flute and said:

"My dear, we must begin at once to educate these poor benighted souls."

"We must," said the lady, earnestly turning from her loom, "we must, indeed. We must take them back to the simple life. It is our mission, our service to humanity— our handing on of the torch."

"Yes," said the gentleman, taking up his flute.

Then he began to play again—so untunefully that even the Outlaws couldn't stand it, and had to retreat to

111

the road. There they discussed the results of their expeditions.

"Lunies," said Ginger, contemptuously, "I bet they've escaped from somewhere."

"They're fun to watch anyway," said William. "We can always come an' watch 'em when we've nothing else to do."

Heartened by the thought of this addition to their resources, they went home to bed.

The next morning they arrived early at the Hall, but there was very little to see. The new-comers were not wearing their flowing robes. They were dressed in their hand-woven tweeds, and they breakfasted (watched by their invisible audience) on barley water and macaroni.

After the meal the man went out, and the Outlaws, after arranging to meet there again that evening, went to school. Somebody, however, gave Ginger a broken air-gun in the course of the morning, and the burning question of its mending occupied the thoughts of the Outlaws to the exclusion of everything else.

They found the air-gun quite unmendable (as Ginger bitterly remarked, "He wouldn't've give it away if it hadn't of been"), but the excitement of taking it to pieces and finding out how it was made almost compensated for this. William, after examining it closely, said that it would be quite easy to make one, and that he meant to set about making one at once.

The attempt absorbed all his energies for the next few days. The result was not successful as an air-gun, but with a little alteration and the addition of a mast and William's handkerchief torn into two pieces for sails, it made quite a good ship of the easily sinkable sort.

The existence of the new tenants of the Hall was

brought back forcibly to his notice by finding the lady of the weaving loom in the drawing-room engaged in returning his mother's call when he returned from experimenting with the new ship in the pond.

The sight rekindled his interest, and after performing a lengthy and laborious toilet (in which he attended to his face, his hands, his knees, his nails, but unfortunately forgot his hair) he entered the drawing-room and greeted the guest with the expression of intense ferocity that he always assumed when he intended to be especially polite. Then he took his seat in a corner of the room.

His mother glanced at him helplessly. He did not usually accord his presence to her drawing-room, and when he did she always suspected that it cloaked some sinister design. Moreover, his hair looked terrible. It stood up wildly around the margins of his face whither his washing operations had driven it.

The visitor, introduced as Mrs. Pennyman, had given him a vague smile and turned at once to his mother again. Evidently his entrance had interrupted an impassioned speech.

"It is the ugliness of modern life," she said, "that shocks Adolphus and me so terribly. The ugliness of the clothes that we have to wear for one thing is repulsive in the extreme. In the evenings, when Adolphus and I are alone at home, we go back to the morning of the world, and wear the clothes that nature intended us to wear."

Seeing a question in Mrs. Brown's eye, Mrs. Pennyman explained hastily, "Flowing robes completely covering the human body and combining beauty with grace and harmony. The world of course is not yet fully educated to them. We have found that we must go slowly and *educate* the world. We tried the experiment of going out in them, but the result was not encouraging. We met with what I can only describe as a hostile reception. We

113

were driven to compromise. In the daytime we wear the ugly garments that convention insists upon, but in the evening, in the seclusion of our own home, we wear the garments that as I said suggest the morning of the world."

"Er—yes," murmured Mrs. Brown, obviously much perplexed by the conversation, "er—yes. Of course."

"And we *weave* everything that we wear," went on Mrs. Pennyman earnestly, "we weave *everything* that we wear with our own *hands*. You see we're going back to the simple life."

"But don't you think," suggested Mrs. Brown tentatively, "that the more modern life's the simpler one? When you don't have to make everything yourself?"

This point of view horrified Mrs. Pennyman.

"Oh, *no*," she said. "Oh, no. Certainly *not*. Simplicity *consists* in—in making things yourself. You see, Adolphus and I feel that we have a *mission*. We want to begin in this little country village, and once the fire is set alight here it will spread like a—like a *network* throughout England. And we want *your* support, dear Mrs. Brown, in setting it alight."

Mrs. Brown looked about her desperately, as if for escape, but all she could see was William gazing at the visitor, with fascinated eyes drinking in her every word. The circle of upstanding hair round his face gave him a startled and slightly sinister look. The sight did not reassure Mrs. Brown, and she wished that her son had given to this visitor as wide a berth as he usually gave to visitors. She tried to turn the conversation on to the weather, but Mrs. Pennyman repeated earnestly:

"May we *count* on your support, dear Mrs. Brown?"

Mrs. Brown gave a non-committal murmur that evidently satisfied her visitor.

"Thank you *so* much," she said. "Every disciple *helps*. . . ."

114

Then she discovered that it was time to go to change into her flowing robes to receive Adolphus.

"I always like him to *find* me dressed in them when he returns from his work. It's so much more pleasant for him. It takes him at *once* back into the morning of the world."

When she had gone, Mrs. Brown looked about for William, but William was not there.

The episode had revived all his interest in the newcomers, and he was behind his screen of laurel watching the returned Mrs. Pennyman, dressed in the classical robe again, struggling with strings of dough that ought to have gone into macaroni but hadn't.

The reformers launched their campaign the next week. They arranged classes in hand-weaving, and they got a lecturer down to speak on "The Reform of Dress," but both were sparsely attended. In fact, the only audience in the latter was a stone deaf old man of Scots descent, who was only there because he attended on principle every village function to which no entrance fee was charged. Next, Mrs. Pennyman gave a lecture on making macaroni, but as drying in the sun was an essential part of the process, and as there wasn't any sun to dry it in, that, too, was a failure, and the mixture had to be made into a loaf which proved too hard for human consumption.

Nothing daunted, the Pennymans got a speaker to lecture upon vegetarianism. The local butcher was the only male member of the audience at this, and he attended in no hostile spirit, but simply because he was curious to see the Pennymans, of whom he had heard so much. He had never seen them before, because in their passage through the village they always made a quarter of a mile *détour* in order to avoid passing his shop.

William, though his life was too full to allow him to

attend the lectures, kept an interested eye upon the proceedings, and still paid frequent unofficial visits to the Hall in order to watch Mr. and Mrs. Pennyman engaged in living the simple life.

He did, as a matter of fact, attend one lecture. It was a lecture given by Mr. Pennyman on "The Evils of Modern Life." He discoursed among other things on the modern tendency of having one's entertainments provided for one, and the joy of entertaining oneself.

As an example of this, Mr. Pennyman played to them on his flute, explaining quite unnecessarily that he had never had any lessons, but had picked it up entirely himself. All the audience, except William, crept out one by one during the recital.

William was present at his unofficial point of observation when the Pennymans sadly decided that they were not getting on with their self-imposed task of Handing on the Torch as fast as they'd hoped to get on, and that they must compromise again.

"Like all reformers we have tried to go too quickly," said Mrs. Pennyman, who was engaged in weaving on her loom a shade of purple that cried aloud to the heavens, "We must *compromise*. We must meet them half-way. We evidently can't take them *straight* back to the morning of the world. We must find some intermediate position and take them there first."

"I know," said Mr. Pennyman, laying aside his hammer (he was engaged this evening in hand beating hand-beaten copper. The sound was rather more tuneful than that of his flute playing). "Merrie England. Let's take them back first to Merrie England."

And so the Merrie England campaign was launched.

It was launched of course with reservations. There wasn't to be any ale (because the Pennymans had very

116

decided views about the effect of strong drink upon the liver), and there wasn't to be any beef. But there was to be milk and nut cutlets. And, of course, there was to be country dancing, accompanied by Mr. Pennyman on his flute. Mrs. Pennyman made smocks and presented them to all the agricultural labourers in the district. Mr. Pennyman made a shepherd's crook of beaten copper, and presented it to the man who looked after the sheep at Jenks' farm. There was quite a large attendance at the first few country dancing classes, but after that a deputation waited upon Mr. and Mrs. Pennyman suggesting that for the remaining classes of the course they should hire a jazz band from the neighbouring country town, and take lessons in the Charleston and the Blues. Mrs. Pennyman fainted over her loom at the suggestion, and Mr. Pennyman nearly swallowed his flute.

"Never!" said Mr. Pennyman dramatically, and Mrs. Pennyman said, still more dramatically, "NEVER!"

So the deputation went away and made arrangements to go into the neighbouring country town once a week to take lessons in ball-room dancing. There were still a fair number left in the country dancing class, however, because there had been rumours of a supper to which all the members were to be invited at the end of the course. They were of that noble kind who had in their childhood doggedly endured the weekly Sunday School for the sake of the annual "treat." But even the Pennymans realised that their campaign lacked "go"; and William, who still could not resist the fascination of the Hall drawing-room, with Mrs. Pennyman weaving and Mr. Pennyman fluting, again formed the unofficial audience when they discussed the situation.

"Things," said Mr. Pennyman, taking the flute from his lips, "aren't progressing as quickly as I'd hoped they would, my dear."

Mrs. Pennyman stooped to disengage her sandal from a clinging mass of soon-to-be hand-woven material. Mrs. Pennyman occasionally got rather tied up in her weaving.

"You are right, Adolphus. We must give them a fillip."

"Have you seen any of the farm labourers wearing the smocks you sent them?"

"I have not, Adolphus. Nor has Jakes once taken out the crook with him as far as I can learn."

"And the country dancing class is smaller than it should be. Everyone in the village should belong to it."

"Have you *told* them so, Adolphus?"

"I have."

"Then tell them again."

"I have told them again."

"It all comes back to the same thing. We must give them a fillip."

"But how, Euphemia?"

For a moment Mrs. Pennyman paced the room in silent thought. In order to assist her meditations Mr. Pennyman raised his flute to his lips and drew from it an unmelodious strain. Mrs. Pennyman silenced him with a gesture.

"I think best in silence, Adolphus," she said. "Music distracts me."

She paced the room in silence several times, watched anxiously by Mr. Pennyman. Then suddenly she stopped and said:

"Of *course!* I *have* it! I *have* it. May Day."

"Yes, my dear," said Mr. Pennyman, looking at her still more anxiously.

"May Day. The first of May. Next month. We must celebrate it. Country dances. A maypole, Morris dancing. A masque. It will give the whole movement a fillip. It will spread from it throughout the whole of England. May Day! The heart and soul of Merrie England! "

Mr. Pennyman rose to his feet reverently and clasped her hand.

"My dear," he said, "you have a wonderful brain."

And so the May Day campaign was launched.

There was to be country dancing, morris dancing, a maypole and a masque. And there were to be free refreshments for the performers. Hearing of the latter the village offered its services in a body. New life and soul entered into the movement. The village green was mown and rolled in preparation for the great day.

William was only vaguely interested in all this. It was the idea of the masque that had gripped his fancy. On hearing it he had had pleasant mental pictures of a gathering of people all wearing comic masks. When he heard that the word meant in this case a play in dumb show his interest waned only to increase to fever point when he heard that it was to represent the fight beween St. George and the dragon.

He gathered that from a conversation that he overheard between Mr. Pennyman and the Vicar. Mr. Pennyman had caught the Vicar as he was slinking into the Vicarage gates with obvious intent of avoiding him. The Pennymans had been grieved to find the Vicar was not quite "sound" on the Merrie England question. He had refused even to promise to be present at the May Day celebrations. He always fled in terror on sight of either of the Pennymans.

But this time Mr. Pennyman caught him very neatly just as he was entering his gate and stood in his path, giving him no chance of escape.

"We hope to see you at our May Day celebrations, Vicar," began Mr. Pennyman very firmly.

The Vicar looked about him in a hunted fashion,

but, finding that Mr. Pennyman barred the only possible way of escape, said:

"Er! —thank you so much, Mr. Pennyman. Delightful, I'm sure. I'm sure it will be delightful. I'm afraid, though, that I may be unable to attend as I may have to go to town to—er—to see—to some urgent business that day. Unfortunate. Most unfortunate. But time and tide, you know. Well, well, I must be——"

"But we shall *expect* you there, Vicar," said Mr. Pennyman firmly. "We shall be *most* disappointed if you fail us. It is to be the beginnings of *great* things for the village."

"I'm sure it will. I'm sure it will," said the Vicar, vainly trying to edge his way past him. "I'm er—*quite* sure it will. Maypole dancing, is it not?"

"That's a part of it," said Mr. Pennyman.

"And a May Queen?"

"Yes," said Mr. Pennyman, "my wife will be the May Queen, of course."

"Er-yes. Delightful," said the Vicar faintly, "simply delightful. I'm so sorry that I shall unfortunately be unable to attend."

"Oh, but you *must* be present, Vicar," said Mr. Pennyman, moving slightly to the left because he saw that the Vicar was trying to get past him on that side. "There's going to be a masque as well as the dancing."

"A masque?" said the Vicar, interested despite himself, because he hadn't heard anything about the masque.

"Yes," said Mr. Pennyman, " a medieval masque. A representation of the fight between St. George and the dragon. I am to be St. George, of course. As a matter of fact I have a suit of armour in which I once went to a fancy dress dance in that very character. There will be a certain suitability too in my taking the part of St. George that I think most people will recognise, because I am giving my life to the struggle against the dark forces of modern life and to bringing back the morning to the world."

"Er-yes," murmured the Vicar. "Delightful," and he edged slightly to the right, but Mr. Pennyman edged also to the right, so the Vicar surrendered himself to fate once more, and said:

"And what about the dragon?"

"I can obtain," said Mr. Pennyman, " a very fine dragon. I refer, of course, to a dragon skin such as is used in pantomimes. Some friends of mine once had it for a child's performance of St. George and the dragon. It may be a little small of course, in comparison with my suit of armour, but I think that it will be quite effective."

"And who," said the Vicar, "will be the dragon?"

"There must be two of them, of course," said Mr. Pennyman. "Two boys, as the thing was made for boys. I haven't really thought about it yet. My nephew who is coming to stay with us for the celebration will be one, of course, and I suppose I must get some local boy to be the other."

At this point the Vicar suddenly noticed William, who, enthralled by the conversation, had drawn so near that he was practically standing between them.

"What do you want, boy?" he snapped irritably.

"Please can you tell me the time?" said William, with admirable presence of mind.

"No, I can't," snapped the Vicar. The incident had thrown Mr. Pennyman off his guard, and the Vicar slipped past him with a murmured farewell, and sped up the drive into the Vicarage with so patent an air of flight that one almost expected to hear him bolt and bar the Vicarage door as soon as he had closed it behind him.

Mr. Pennyman turned and walked up the road to the Hall in the gathering dusk followed by William. Mr.

"What do you want, boy?" the Vicar asked irritably

Pennyman was thinking that it didn't really matter if the Vicar didn't turn up for the May Day celebrations. There was nothing medieval or picturesque or romantic about him. You couldn't, for instance, dress him in a smock or give him a shepherd's crook. No, if the Vicar wanted to go up to town on May Day, he could. They could manage perfectly well without him. Better than with him probably.

He walked up the drive of the Hall, unaware that William was still following closely on his heels, entered the front door and closed it behind him. He joined his wife in the drawing-room. She threw him a pained look.

"Adolphus," she said, "do go and change out of those horrible clothes. You don't look like *my* Adolphus in them. . . ."

"I will in a minute, dearest," he said apologetically. "I just wanted to tell you that I saw the Vicar——"

The housemaid entered and said:

"There's a boy wants to see you, sir."

"A boy?" said Mr. Pennyman. "What sort of a boy? What does he want?"

"He says he's come about the dragon, sir."

"The what?" said Mr. Pennyman.

"That's what he said, sir," said the maid dispassionately. "He said he'd come about the dragon."

"What dragon?"

"He didn't say, sir. He just said he'd come about the dragon."

"How mysterious! " said Mrs. Pennyman. "You'd better show him in."

Almost immediately William entered. He wore his most ferocious scowl.

"I've come about the dragon," he began unceremoniously.

"What dragon?" said Mr. Pennyman.

"The dragon you're going to have. I want to be its front legs."

"Oh-er, I see. But who told you about it?"

Mr. Pennyman who was short-sighted did not recognise William as the boy who had asked the Vicar the time.

"Oh, I—I jus' sort of heard," said William.

Mr. and Mrs. Pennyman had drawn nearer to William and were looking at him critically. Then, one on each side of him, they discussed him over his head, William staring in front of him with a completely expressionless face.

"He's—not *quite* the type we want, surely, dear," said Mr. Pennyman anxiously.

"His face won't show," said his wife.

"True," said Mr. Pennyman, "true. Of course his face won't show."

"And of course his motives are very important. If he does it in the right spirit, and—of course, his face won't show. Why do you want to take the part, boy? Is it because you want to help in the task of taking back this village to Merrie England, and thence to the morning of the world."

"Yes," said William.

"It's an excellent motive, of course," said Mr. Pennyman. "It seems a pity not to encourage it. My little nephew Pelleas has offered to take one of the parts of the animal. He may want the front legs. Perhaps you would take the back?"

"I'd rather take the front," said William very firmly, and still with a face expressionless to the verge of imbecility, added: " 'Cause of what you said just now about the morning in the world and such-like."

Mrs. Pennyman was touched.

"Clouds of glory!" she said. "How wonderful! Prob-

124

ably in spite of his face he has a beautiful soul. But of course Pelleas too understands and appreciates our message. Pelleas will be with us to-morrow, dear boy. So will you come here then at four o'clock, and we will decide between you."

William arrived at the Hall promptly the next afternoon and was shown into the drawing-room. Pelleas was there with Mrs. Pennyman. Pelleas was about William's age and height, but he was dressed in a Kate Greenaway suit, and his hair was too long. Mrs. Pennyman waved her hand towards William, and said to Pelleas: "This is the boy who's going to be the other half of the dragon, Pelleas."

Pelleas subjected William to a lengthy scrutiny.

"I don't like him," he said at length. "He's ugly."

"But, darling," said Mrs. Pennyman, "his *face* won't show, you know."

"It will to me if we're both inside the dragon."

"It won't, darling, because it'll be dark."

"Well I don't like him, anyway," said Pelleas firmly, "and I don't want to be a dragon with him."

"We'll see what your uncle says," said Mrs. Pennyman vaguely.

Mr. Pennyman entered just then and said that he would try them both in the skin to see which did the front legs best.

"But I don't want to be a dragon with him at all," expostulated Pelleas. "I don't like him. He's a nasty, ugly boy. I've been brought up to love beautiful things about me."

"He can't help his appearance," said Mr. Pennyman, "and he's a good earnest boy. He's eager to help to bring back the morning of the world."

"I don't care," said Pelleas.

William, anxious to be tried as the dragon's legs, maintained his expressionless expression though there was a gleam in his eye whenever it rested on Pelleas.

Mr. Pennyman took them both upstairs to the attic where the dragon's skin was kept. It was a wonderful dragon's skin, long and green and shiny with glaring eyes and a ferocious open mouth displaying a curving tongue and sharp white teeth. It made William gasp with delight. He knew that unless he were the front legs of this creature life would turn to dust and ashes in his mouth. Mr. Pennyman fetched his sword and they rehearsed the fight. At first they tried Pelleas as the front legs and William as the hind legs, but Pelleas screamed as soon as he caught sight of Mr. Pennyman's sword and said: "Go away. I'll tell my mother. Go away," whenever Mr. Pennyman advanced upon him flourishing it. The engagement between them was unworthy of the name of combat, and so William and Pelleas changed places. William took the front legs and Pelleas the back. And William was superb. He roared and hissed and bellowed. He flung himself upon Mr. Pennyman most realistically, then retired as if beaten back by Mr. Pennyman's gleaming sword. He crouched and sprang and retreated again, and finally, on receiving the death blow, he writhed and struggled with such effect that Mr. Pennyman, who hadn't really wanted him to be the front legs, dropped his sword and cried "bravissimo."

So it was arranged that William was to be the front legs and Pelleas the back ones. Pelleas, on hearing the decision, said:

"I don't care. He'll prob'ly get excited an' stick his sword right through you an' kill you an' I shan't care if he does either."

There was a right merry scene on May Day on the

village green. All the village was assembled, smocks were much in evidence, and the postman had been persuaded to carry the shepherd's crook.

Great trestle tables at one end of the green groaned beneath the weight of flagons of milk and dishes piled high with nut cutlets and protein sandwiches. The Vicar had sent a note regretting that he could not be present, and saying that important business took him up to town.

The performance opened by the crowning of Mrs. Pennyman as Queen of the May to the strains of Mr. Pennyman's flute. Next followed a maypole dance, for which also Mr. Pennyman played on his flute. This was not an unqualified success. Some ribbons got left out altogether; and others got finished up before the thing was half-way through. Moreover, Mrs. Pennyman, who was enthroned within the circle close to the pole in her character of Queen of the May, got entangled in the ribbons and nearly throttled but they managed to get her out alive, and being a true optimist she said with her first returning breath that the dance had been a great success.

Then followed the interval during which a dejected-looking group gathered round the refreshment table, and tried the milk and nut cutlets, to disperse almost immediately looking still more dejected.

Then came the masque of St. George and the dragon. A small hut had been provided as a green room, and from it now issued Mr. Pennyman clad in bright armour and followed by his dragon. The spectators formed a ring, and St. George and the dragon walked round it twice, the dragon's front legs frisking and curveting in such an undignified fashion that St. George more than once had to rebuke it.

Then they faced each other in the ring for the fight. William was just preparing his roar when Pelleas, in whose heart the sense of inferiority that appertains to the hind legs had been rankling ever since the part had been assigned him, said:

"Best place for you, inside a dragon where people can't see you."

"Think so?" said William, foolishly staying to bandy abuse instead of charging his knight.

"Yes I do."

"Well, I'd rather look like what I do that what you do."

"Oh, you would, would you, Monkey Brand?"

"Yes, I would, little Lord Fauntleroy."

Neither knew which began it, but suddenly to the amazement of the onlookers the dragon seemed to be taken by a sort of internal spasm. It appeared, in fact, to be writhing in mortal agony. Its front legs and hind legs were fighting. St. George, awaiting its arranged onset, was for a moment nonplussed. Then, realising that as it would not fight him he must fight it, he flung himself upon it rather more heavily than he meant to because he slipped and clutched at it to save himself from falling. William, engaged in a desperate struggle with Pelleas inside the skin, suddenly found himself attacked in the rear. Forgetful of everything else he turned in a fury to repel this fresh attack and the knight found himself suddenly hurled on to the ground. His armour was so arranged upon him that once on his knees he could not rise from them. His enraged dragon, however, seemed still to be advancing upon him with hostile intent, so he began to crawl as best he could to a place of safety. The spectators then beheld the glorious sight of St. George pursued round the ring on all fours by a ferocious dragon, and finally taking refuge from it in the green room hut. Their depression vanished as if by magic.

A deafening cheer went up. Merrie England seemed at last to have arrived.

The Pennymans left the neighbourhood almost immediately afterwards. They said that it was not worthy of the torch.

Most of the villagers held for the rest of their lives a mistaken conception of the issue of the fight between St. George and the dragon, but they always looked back to the day of the masque with feelings of pleasure.

William's only feeling on the matter was one of regret that he never really finished the fight with Pelleas.

William and the Over-Ten Club

"NOW hurry up with your breakfast, William," said Mrs. Brown, "and do try to eat properly."

There was a wistful note in her voice. Usually she looked forward to a few minutes' peace after Mr. Brown's whirlwind departure for the station to catch his morning train, but William's school holidays had begun and it was difficult to reconcile William's presence with an atmosphere of peace.

"And Mrs. Peters isn't coming this morning," she added, "so I shall have a lot to do."

William, his brows drawn into a purposeful frown, continued to pour milk into the moat of a porridge fortress that sagged in the middle of his plate.

"This porridge isn't thick enough," he complained. "I can't make any battlements. 'Least, they keep floppin' over. An' I can't get the drawbridge to stand up prop'ly either. . . . Why isn't she comin'?"

129

F

"Because she's going on a coach ride to the sea with the Over-Sixty Club. Do stop messing about with your food, William."

"I'm not messin'. . . . The moat's overflowed its banks. Well, I bet that'll keep enemies off all right even if the drawbridge *has* splodged right down in the middle of it. I'll pretend a tank's gone over it an' crashed right through it, hurtling to its doom in the raging torrent below. . . .Can I have a piece of sugar for the tank, please?"

"No, William. Eat your porridge if you want it and leave it if you don't."

"I do want it. I'm goin' to eat it now. This spoon's a jet bomber swoopin' down on the fortress." He emitted a nerve-shattering sound, then looked earnestly at his mother. "Did that sound like a jet bomber?"

"I don't know," said Mrs. Brown faintly, "but don't do it again."

"All right," said William and continued, in a voice muffled by two battlements and a drawbridge, "Gosh! An' she went to the pictures with 'em las' Monday an' she went out to tea with 'em the Monday before."

"Yes, Sir Gerald and Lady Markham kindly asked them all to tea at Marleigh Manor . . . Now, William, have you finished?"

"Nearly."

William disposed of the remainder of the porridge with an abstracted air, obviously no longer interested in the aerial assault.

"Gosh! " he said as he laid down his spoon. "They get everythin' done for them."

"Who gets everything done for them? Here's a sausage for you if you want it."

"Thanks. Why do they always make sausages the same shape? If I made 'em I'd make 'em all diff'rent shapes.

130

I'd make some like ships an' some like trains an' some like aeroplanes an' some like——"

"Do hurry, William. I want to start the washing-up."

"All right. I'll hurry now. . . . The old."

"What on earth are you talking about, dear?"

"The old," repeated William sombrely. "They get everythin' done for them. Old Age Pensions an' Over-Sixty Clubs an' everythin'. It isn't fair. I tried to get Young Age Pensions fixed up once but no one'd listen to me. Why shouldn't we have Young Age Pensions same as they have Old Age Pensions? It jus' isn't fair."

"Don't be so silly, dear, and fold up your table napkin if you've finished."

"They jus' get paid for bein' old. Well, what I say is, why shun't we get paid for bein' young, same as they get paid for bein' old? What's the diff'rence?"

"I said *fold* it, William, not screw it into creases like that. People naturally want to do all they can to cheer up the old."

"Well, why don't they want to do all they can to cheer up the young?" said William, shaking out his table napkin and screwing it into a fresh assortment of creases. "I bet the young need cheerin' up a jolly sight more than what the old do. The old don't have to go to school every day, wearin' out their brains with mental torcher over Latin an' sums an' things. I wrote to the gov'n'ment about Young Age Pensions but they never answered. An' now this Over-Sixty Club! Goin' off to the seaside an' pictures an' tea parties! They jus' get *everythin'* done for them. . . . Can I scrape out the honey, please? It's nearly finished."

"There's quite a lot left in it, William. . . . Oh, very well. And you can give me a hand with putting the things on the trolley, if you like."

"Yes, I will," said William through a mouthful of

honey. "Why don't we keep bees? I'd look after 'em. They eat flowers an' there's lots of flowers about, so they wouldn't cost anythin' to feed. Not like dog biscuits an' ants' eggs. An' I bet I could teach them tricks." He stacked up a pile of plates and saucers adding a leaning tower of cups which was only saved from collapse by Mrs. Brown's presence of mind.

"William! Do be more careful. Put the things on the trolley one by one. . . . Of course we can't keep bees and it's only natural that people should want to help the old and be careful with that sugar basin. You'll have it all over the trolley waving it about like that. There! I knew you would! If you're going to help, do try to give your mind to it."

William tried to give his mind to it, but his thoughts were still busy with his grievances.

"Jus' think of those old Over-Sixty people goin' swimmin' in the sea while we're doin' rotten old sums an' g'ography! Can I wheel the trolley into the kitchen now?"

"I don't suppose that any of them go swimming in the sea," said Mrs. Brown, recoiling from a mental picture of her "daily help" in swimming costume, "and be careful with the trolley . . . There! I knew you were going to bang it into the kitchen table."

"Sorry. There's only a bit of milk gone on the floor. I'll wipe it up."

"Not with the tea-towel, William!"

"All right! I'll use this duster."

"That's *not* a duster, William. It's a tray-cloth."

"Sorry . . . Listen! Who started all these Over-Sixty Clubs an' things, anyway?"

"I suppose someone just thought of it and did it. Now, William, don't put the loaf in the fridge."

"Sorry . . . I was thinkin' of somethin' else. . . . I s'pose anyone can starts clubs anywhere?"

"I suppose so. Look! I knew you were going to spill that honey. Now, it's all over the dresser."

"'S all right. I can lick it off. . . . Shall I wash up for you now?"

"No, thank you, dear."

"But I want to help you now Mrs. Peters has gone off swimmin' in the sea."

"No, thank you, dear," said Mrs. Brown, adding hopefully: "Isn't there anything you'd rather be doing somewhere else?"

"Well, axshully, there is," said William, "an' I *have* helped, haven't I?"

"Yes, dear."

"Well, I'll go now if you're sure you can manage without me."

"I'm quite sure, dear."

"All right. I'll go an' find Ginger an' Henry an' Douglas."

He plunged upstairs to his bedroom and returned, sliding down the banisters and landing noisily on the floor at the bottom. His untuneful whistle dispelled from the countryside the last lingering traces of its early morning hush as he set off down the road.

Mrs. Brown threw a harassed glance at the sugar on the trolley, the milk on the floor, the honey on the dresser, and the trail of small oddments of cutlery that marked the passage of the trolley from dining-room to kitchen . . . then set herself briskly to the work of clearing up.

William had collected Ginger, Henry and Douglas and was holding forth to them eloquently as they made their way towards the old barn.

"They get money an' rides to the seaside an' pictures an' theatres an' tea parties an'—an' everythin' *given* to

*"You're only nine, Arabella Simpkin," said
William sternly*

134

'em jus' 'cause they're old. Think of 'em all swimmin' in the sea an' we've not been to the seaside since—since —well, since, the las' time we went. It's not fair an' somethin' ought to be done about it."

"What *can* be done about it?" said Ginger, retrieving from the ditch a fragment of a branch that had been blown down in a recent gale and flourishing it in the manner of a walking stick.

"Well, I'm tired of writing to the gov'n'ment," said William. "I've never had an answer yet. Huh!" He gave his short sarcastic laugh. "Seems to me this old Minister of Old Age Pensions, whoever he is, has got so old he's

135

forgot how to write. Anyway, when we get a Minister of Young Age Pensions——"

"I bet we never will," said Douglas gloomily. "I bet the Black Rod or the Head of the Opposition or some-one'll stop us."

" 'Course we'll get one," said William. "I'll be him myself when I'm grown up, an' then I'll get things goin' a bit better than what they are now."

"I don't see how you're goin' to find time for all the things you're goin' to be," said Henry, "inventor, an' air pilot an' diver an' fireman an' sweet-shop man an' engine-driver an' now Minister of Young Age Pensions."

"Oh, I'll get 'em in all right," said William airily. "They're all jolly easy things to do once you get into the way of them."

"An' if we've got to wait till you're grown up before we get anythin' done, it won't be much good to us," said Douglas.

"Well, we won't have to wait," said William. "We'll have to wait for Young Age Pensions, of course, but we needn't wait for things like Over-Sixty Clubs. We could start that straight away."

"What's the use of an Over-Sixty Club to us?" said Douglas. "It'll be years an' years before we get to be over sixty."

"Don't be such a chump," said William. "We wouldn't have it over sixty. We'd have it our age. We'd have——" He paused to consider. "We'd have—— Yes, we'd have an Over-Ten Club. We're all over ten, so we could have an Over-Ten Club easy. Then we could have a jolly good time goin' to pictures an' theatres an' tea parties an' having coach rides to the sea."

"Yes, but how are we goin' to *get* 'em—pictures an' tea parties an' things?" said Henry, who was of a prac-tical turn of mind.

"Oh, we won't bother about that jus' yet," said William, waving the question aside impatiently. "*They* get 'em so I don't see why we shouldn't. I bet it's quite easy to fix up. The first thing to do is to get this Over-Ten Club started."

"An' how're you goin' to do it?" said Ginger, leaning heavily upon his stick and falling to the ground as it collapsed beneath his weight. "I bet it's not as easy as all that, startin' clubs."

" 'Course it is," said William, giving Ginger's mishap the tribute of a derisive chuckle. "We'll put up a notice on the door of the old barn. I bet people'll join all right when we tell em' all the excitin' things they're goin' to do."

"Yes, it's not the joinin' part that's worryin' me," said Ginger, brushing himself down and throwing away the remnants of his stick. "Must have had dry rot in it or this death clock beetle what churches get. It looked all right . . . What's worrying me is what's goin' to happen after they've joined."

"If everyone was like you," said William severely, "no one'd ever have discovered anythin'—not America nor—nor fountain pens nor anythin'."

"I think it's goin' to be a waste of time," said Douglas. "I'd rather be playin' Lions an' Tamers."

"Yes, it's a good game, is Lions an' Tamers," said William reflectively, adding: "P'raps we could work it into the Over-Ten Club, once we get it goin'."

"Lions and Tamers" was strongly disapproved of by the Outlaws' mothers but it was a game that the Outlaws had played ever since they could remember. Although there were long periods when it sank into disuse, they would revive it at regular intervals, playing it in season and out of season with such abandon that it was generally forbidden again by Authority before they had had time

137

to tire of it. It was essentially a simple game without complicated rules—indeed without any rules at all. Half the players were lions and half were tamers. The tamers tried to tame the lions and the lions resisted the tamers' efforts with all the ferocity they could muster. It was a game with no formal beginning and no formal end. The players began it when their high spirits felt the need of immediate outlet and stopped when they were too much exhausted to continue.

"But we've gotter get the club goin' first," said William. "Come on. Let's write out the notice for the meetin' an see how many of 'em turn up."

The notice was composed by William, written by Ginger and edited by Douglas, who altered the spelling of "president" from "pressidunt" to "prezidant" and put in an occasional comma. In order to give it an official air, Henry had printed the words "Countie Burrow of Hadley" in red ink at the top and affixed a three-half-penny stamp taken from the envelope of a circular that he had found in the waste-paper basket at home.

It read:

Nottis Ergunt.

overtenn klub

Their will, be a meating tomorrough afternun of peeple over, tenn to gett up an overtenn, klub ennyone, over-tenn kan kum not, annimuls William Brown prezidant will maik a speach peeple, that interrupp him will, be chuckd out

cined William Brown

The attendance at the meeting was gratifying, though the "over ten" qualification seemed to have been largely ignored. As usual the entire juvenile population of the village flocked to the old barn, headed by Arabella Simpkin, wheeling her baby brother in a ramshackle pram, and wearing a moth-eaten fur and a ragged eye-veil (both

138

belonging to her mother) in order to lend her an air of maturity.

"You're only nine, Arabella Simpkin," said William sternly. "So you can jolly well clear out."

"You shut up, William Brown," said Arabella Simpkin haughtily. "Always poking your nose into things what aren't your business."

"It *is* my business," said William. "I'm gettin' up this club an' it's for over-ten people, not for kids like you."

Arabella gave a shrill laugh.

"D'you think I *want* to b'long to your rotten ole club, William Brown? Huh! Fancy you thinkin' I want to b'long to your rotten ole club!"

"All right, go home then," said William. "You're nine an' we don't want kids of nine."

Arabella repeated the shrill laugh.

"Fancy you thinkin' I'm only nine, William Brown! You *are* ig'rant."

"How old are you, then?" challenged William.

"I'm—I'm sixteen," said Arabella defiantly, tossing the string of moth-eaten fur about her neck and fingering the eye-veil with such a fierce gesture that it slipped its moorings on her school beret and came down over her mouth.

There was a murmur of expostulation.

"Oo, you story teller!"

"Oo, you're nine. I *know* you're nine."

"She was eight las' year an' seven the year before, so she *mus'* be nine. Oo, isn't she a story teller?"

Realising that the feeling of the assembly was against her on this point, Arabella shifted her attack to more general grounds.

"Who d'you think you are, William Brown, bossing people round? King of the Cannibal Isles, I shouldn't wonder!"

"Chuck her out!" said Henry.

"Yes, you try!" shrilled Arabella, standing arms akimbo and sucking her eye-veil furiously. "Jus' you *try* chuckin' me out!"

"Well, look at him," said William, pointing to the baby and shifting his line of attack in his turn. "What's he doin' here, anyway? You can't say *he's* over ten."

The baby stared at William dispassionately for a few moments then bent his whole attention to the work of blowing bubbles with his saliva.

"He's two," chorused the meeting. "We know he's two 'cause his mother says so. An' Arabella's nine 'cause we *know* she is."

A smile of triumph curved Arabella's thin lips.

"Well, that makes us a person of eleven between us, doesn't it? So we can b'long. We can b'long as a person of eleven, so *there,* William Brown!"

"Gosh! You can't do that," said William, taken aback.

"There's nothin' in the notice to say you can't," said Arabella, "an' I'm goin' to. We're a person of eleven— our Fred an' me—an' you can't stop us joinin' your ole club, so there!"

William would have liked to continue the argument but the meeting was growing restive.

"Well, come on," said a small stocky child with beetling brows and a mouth that showed determination, despite the liquorice bootlace that dangled from it. "Is anythin' goin' to happen or isn't it?"

"Yes, it is, if you'll all shut up a minute," said William, mounting the packing case that served him as a platform. "If you'll all shut up a minute an' listen I'm goin' to make a speech."

A ragged cheer of mingled applause and derision arose.

"Now listen to me," said William, raising his voice

140

above the uproar. "Kin'ly listen to me. I'm goin' to start makin' this speech. Ladies an' gentlemen——"

Another ragged cheer arose, through which Arabella's voice could be heard saying with shrill sarcasm: "I mus' be blind. I don't see no gentlemen."

"Shut up, Arabella Simpkin," said William. "Now listen to me, everybody. I'm the president an' I'm makin' this speech. Now listen." The murmurs died away. "There's a club called the Over-Sixty Club what people over sixty belong to an' they have a jolly good time jus' 'cause they're over sixty, an' what I say is I don't see why we shouldn't have a jolly good time jus' 'cause we're over ten. There's lors that people shouldn't be punished for things that aren't their fault an' it's not our fault we're not over sixty an' even if we *tried* to be over sixty we couldn't 'cause you can't be over sixty if you're not over sixty by nacher so it's not fair an' something ought to be done about it."

A confused babble arose as the audience awoke to a sense of its grievances.

"Let's go an' give 'em a bashin'," said a small angelic-looking boy with large blue eyes and blond hair.

"Let's dress up as over sixty with beards an' things," said Frankie Parker. "I could borrow my grandmother's ear trumpet. She'd jus' think she'd lost it. She's always losin' it."

"There's a ninvalid chair in our garage what my great uncle used to drive, but I dunno how to drive it."

"There's two walking sticks as home. I could use 'em, same as crutches."

"Why not wait till we get to be over sixty?" suggested a placid-looking child who was licking a toffee apple. "Everyone gets to be over sixty if they wait long enough. It only wants a bit of patience."

"I'd like to see William Brown sixty," jeered Arabella.

141

"Gosh! He'll be worth lookin' at. He's a sight to start with."

"Shut up, Arabella Simpkin," said William. "Shut up, everyone. Now listen to me, all of you. I'm goin' to go on makin' this speech. Shut up an' listen to me goin' on makin' this speech." The uproar died away again to a few murmurings. "I'm goin' to start it again from the beginnin'. Ladies an' gentlemen, those old over-sixties get everythin' done for them an' I bet it's time we had somethin' done for us an' I'm goin' to start an Over-Ten Club an' all of you that's over ten can b'long an' we'll have tea parties an' cinemas an' rides to the seaside same as what they do." A loud cheer arose. "Anyone what wants to join put their hands up."

A forest of hands arose.

"They can't all join," said Henry. "Some of 'em are jus' children. I bet that more'n half of them aren't over ten."

"Well, it's no good tryin' to sort 'em out," said Douglas. "We'd only get in a muddle."

"We'll sort 'em out later," said William. "We've got to get it fixed up prop'ly first."

But the club seemed to consider itself fixed up properly already. They swarmed round William eagerly, expectantly, with a touching trust and confidence.

"Come on, William!"

"What'll we do first, William?"

"Let's go to the pictures.'

"Let's go to the seaside."

"No, let's have a tea party, William."

William was a little disconcerted by the immediate success of his scheme.

"We can't do anythin' straight away," he temporised. "We—well, we've got to think things out a bit first. I

142

dunno that we can do anythin' jus' now. Not jus' this minute. I mean—well, I mean——"

They interrupted him with indignant protests.

"You *said* we could go to the pictures."

"You *promised* we could go to the seaside."

"I want to go *now!*"

"Huh!" jeered Arabella. "Might've known William Brown couldn't do nothin' but make speeches. Not much of a speech neither, he didn't make. Our Fred here could make a better speech than what he did, any day."

As if to prove this point, Fred raised his voice in a prolonged howl. Through the howl the protests continued.

"Calling himself King of the Cannibal Isles an' can't even take people to the seaside."

"I never did," said William.

"Where's this tea party you kept talkin' about?"

"Oh, he can *talk* all right," said Arabella. "He can make as much noise as a donkey but he can't *do* nothin'. That's him all over."

"You *can* do somethin', can't you, William?"

"Reg'lar swindle, that's what it is," said Arabella, tossing the moth-eaten fur over her shoulder with such *élan* that it landed on the ground a few yards behind her.

"Oughter be in prison, that's where he ought to be."

"You *can* take us somewhere, can't you, William?"

"'Course I can," said William. "'Course I can, an' you can jolly well shut up, Arabella Simpkin. What d'you think I started this club for if I couldn't? Come on!"

Cheers greeted this pronouncement and, before William quite knew what was happening, he found himself walking across the fields towards Hadley, his Over-Ten Club clamouring excitedly at his heels.

"The pictures!"

"Let's go to the pictures."

"Gosh! Isn't it smashing! William's takin' us to the pictures."

William's faint disclaimers were drowned in the uproar and in less than a minute, as it seemed to him, he was being propelled along Hadley's main street towards Hadley's main cinema.

At the door he turned to survey the rag, tag and bobtail that comprised his Over-Ten Club. Fortunately the disgrace of the pram had been removed. (Arabella's mother had indignantly retrieved it on its reckless passage through the village), but Arabella still headed the crowd, her fur perched precariously on her shoulder, her eye-veil dangling in a drunken fashion from one corner of her school beret.

"You'd better wait out here while I go in an' fix it up," said William in a tone of authority that did not quite conceal an underlying nervousness. "Count 'em, Ginger. How many of them are there?"

"About nineteen, I think," said Ginger. "I can't count 'em all 'cause they keep movin' about."

A small boy was running excitedly in and out of the others and a little girl was hopping up and down the steps that led to the entrance, singing "Polly Wolly Doodle," in a shrill tuneless voice. The commissionaire eyed them with mingled apprehension and distaste.

"Well, go on, William Brown," said Arabella. "How much longer are you goin' to keep us hangin' round?"

"All right, all right," said William. "I've gotter have time to breathe, haven't I, same as everyone else."

He mounted the steps and approached the pay desk in a nonchalant fashion.

"Nineteen one-an'-sixpennies," he said to the man at the desk.

The man at the desk stared at him.

"Where's your money?" he said.

144

"I haven't any," said William. "We don't pay. We're the Over-Ten Club."

"The—*what*?" said the man.

"The Over-Ten Club," explained William patiently. "Same as the Over-Sixty Club. We go into things free."

"You——?" For a moment the man's indignation deprived him of speech. Then it returned. "Out you go, my lad, and quicker than you came in and if I have any more of your monkey tricks——"

There was something in his tone that made William turn hurriedly towards the exit. His Over-Ten Club closed round him eagerly.

"Is it all right, William?"

"Can we go in now, William?"

"No," said William. "No, it's—it's not a good film. You wouldn't like it. I had a good look at the pictures of it an'—well, it's a jolly dull film. You wouldn't like it. I said we wouldn't go to it, 'cause it's such a jolly dull film."

There was a murmur of disappointment.

"I wouldn't mind," said the stocky little girl with beetling brows. "I like dull films."

The commissionaire was bearing down threateningly upon them and William set off hastily along the street, followed by his motley crew.

"What are we goin' to do, William?"

"Let's go to the seaside, shall we, William?"

"Look! " shrilled Arabella, pointing with a small claw-like hand across the street.

Outside a tobacconist-and-sweetshop stood a large notice.

"Daily outings to Brighton, Worthing, Hastings."

An eager clamour arose from the Over-Ten Club.

"The seaside! "

"Look, William, we can go to the seaside now."

"Come on quick! Let's go to the seaside."

"Well—er—you'd better wait here, while I fix it up," said William, goaded into action despite his misgivings. "You wait here while I go across an' fix it up."

"Yes, same as you did las' time," taunted Arabella. "You fixed it up jolly well las' time, didn't you! I s'pose you'll be sayin' it's a dull seaside or somethin' like that. Trust you to make a mess of it, William Brown."

"You wait! " said William. "You jus' wait an' see. I'll go across now an' I bet it'll be all right."

He crossed the street and entered the shop. A bored-looking youth with long hair and a receding chin came forward.

"We—er—we want to go to the seaside," said William. Surprise invaded the boredom of the young man's face.

"We?" he said.

"Yes," said William. "About twenty of us."

"You mean—you wish to charter a coach?"

"Yes," said William.

"When do you wish to go?"

"Now," said William.

Suspicion struggled with surprise in the young man's face.

"I could fix you up tomorrow . . ."

"All right," said William. "Tomorrow'd do. We can put it off till tomorrow all right."

"You'll pay a deposit, I take it?"

"No," said William, "we don't pay anythin'. We go free. We're the Over Ten-Club. Same as the Over-Sixty Club, you know."

His friends watched his summary ejection from the shop with mild surprise. He had regained something of his aplomb, however, when he rejoined them.

"You came out jolly quick," said Ginger.

146

"Yes," said William. "I was in a bit of a hurry an' I didn't want to waste any more time talkin' to him."

"What about goin' to the seaside, William?"

"Can we start now, William?"

"Can I catch a crab, William?"

"Can I jus' run home to fetch my bucket an' spade, William?"

"Well, you see," said William, "I'm sorry about it, but it's—it's jolly cold at the seaside jus' now. You wouldn't enjoy it. 'S no good goin' to things you wouldn't enjoy. So I told him we wouldn't go . . . 'S no good goin' if it's cold. I b'lieve it's rainin' at the seaside, as well. Snowin', too, I shouldn't wonder."

Their excitement changed again to disappointment.

"What can we do, then, William?"

"What about that tea party, William? Will you take us to that tea party, if we can't go to the pictures or the seaside?"

"Er—yes," said William. He felt as if he were in the grip of one of those nightmares from which one longs unavailingly to awake. "Oh, yes, a little thing like a party's nothin' to me. Huh!"

They straggled on down the street.

"I dunno . . ." said William hoarsely. "I mean . . . I wonder . . . I mean, p'haps we'd better put it off a bit till I've got somethin' better fixed up."

Resentful murmurs arose.

"I want a tea party if I can't go to the seaside."

"You *promised* us a tea party, William."

"I'd have *liked* that dull film, William."

"I wouldn't have minded if it *was* snowin' at the seaside, William."

"I'm getting ever so hungry, William. Where *is* this tea party?"

"Will there be chocolate biscuits, William?"

William and his band rushed into the room

"Are we nearly there, William?"

Arabella's voice rose shrilly over the murmurs.

"I b'lieve there ain't no tea party, neither. Huh! It'll be snowin' at the tea party same as at the seaside. He'll get out of it somehow. A reg'lar swindler, he is. He ought to be shut up in the Tower same as the ones in hist'ry."

148

"Jus' you *wait*," said the goaded William. "Jus' you wait till you get to this party. You'll be jolly well surprised when you get to it."

"Yes, we'll be s'prised if anythin' happens. . . ."

But just then something did happen. They were passing a large building at the door of which stood a small harassed-looking woman. Her face broke into smiles of welcome as her eyes lit on William and his band.

"Oh, there you are, children! We were so afraid you wouldn't be able to get here. Come along in."

The children swarmed into the room. At one end several elderly people sat dejectedly round little tables. At the other end a large trestle table was laden with cakes, jellies, chocolate biscuits and other dainties.

"I'm Miss Fountain, children," said the lady, "and when Miss Mirabel rang up this morning to say that the fog was so thick in London that she didn't think you'd be able to come I was terribly disappointed, but I still clung to the hope that it would clear and that you'd come, after all, and, you see"—she laughed gaily—"I was right. I had one of my *feelings* that you'd come and they very seldom mislead me. Come along . . . I knew that you'd be hungry after your journey, so I thought I'd give you a nice tea before you began your dancing. I've been reading extracts from Tennyson aloud to our Over-Sixties and, though I'm sure they've enjoyed it, no doubt they'll be glad of a change. . . . Miss Mirabel's not come with you, I see."

"No," said William, feeling that some answer was expected.

"Oh, well, I suppose you know what to do. She said that it was a particularly busy week for her. What about your costumes? Have you brought them with you?"

"No," said William.

"Oh, dear! She said that a friend would be bringing them separately in her car, but no doubt the fog has delayed things. I suppose that you can dance just as well without them?"

"Yes," said William, still following the line of least resistance.

The others were not listening to the conversation. They had taken their seats at the table and were already hard at work on the feast. William made haste to join them and they greeted him with cries of delight.

"Oo, William, it's lovely! "

"It's a *real* tea party."

"Oo, *look* at that pink cake! "

"An' that red jelly."

"Oo, William, it's better than the pictures."

Even Arabella found time to remark grudgingly through a mouthful of jam sandwich: "Well, you've not made a muddle over *this*, William Brown, I mus' say."

Miss Fountain was addressing the depressed-looking gathering at the other end of the room.

"You'll all be glad to know that Miss Mirabel's Juveniles have managed to get here, after all. Without Miss Mirabel and without their costumes, I'm afraid, but I'm sure you won't mind that. We'll enjoy their beautiful dancing just as much in everyday clothes. . . . I won't continue the Tennyson reading in the circumstances——"

A faint cheer arose from her audience and she gave them a gratified smile.

"I'm so glad you enjoyed it. And now I'll go and see how the Juveniles are getting on."

Neither William nor any of his band had listened to the speech. They were busy clearing up the remnants of the feast, disposing of the last crumbs of cakes, sandwiches and biscuits, the last shreds of jelly and trifle. Then William noticed that Miss Fountain was hovering anxiously about him.

"You're in charge of the Juveniles, aren't you, dear?" she said.

"Yes," said William.

"Well, perhaps, if you've all finished your tea you'd get them started, would you, dear? I don't know whether you want music, do you, dear?"

"No, thanks," said William. "No, we don't want music."

"Such a good thing, because, though there is a piano and I do play a little, I'm not very sure of the notes and actually only certain of the notes on this particular instrument give out any sound at all, so, as I suppose that Miss Mirabel generally plays for you and as she couldn't come with you, perhaps it would be best to dispense with music altogether." Being an optimistic woman, she mistook William's stare of blank bewilderment for a look of intelligence and continued: "Well, you'll see to it all, won't you dear? We've left a good clear space for you."

She went to the other end of the room and took her place among the Over-Sixties, watching William and his Over-Tens with an expectant smile.

"Well, we've had a jolly good tea," said Arabella, still grudgingly approving, as she retrieved the eye-veil (which had lost its moorings in the general excitement and fallen limply into her tea-cup), and fastened it, sodden and shapeless, over her beret with an air of exaggerated elegance. "An' what'll we do now?"

William had ceased wrestling with his bewilderment. Fate had mysteriously led him to this place, provided him with a lavish tea and set apart a clear expanse of floor.

"Let's have a game," he said.

"What game?" they clamoured eagerly.

"Lions an' Tamers," said William.

"Oh, goody, goody!" cried the Over-Tens, leaping exultantly from their seats. "Show us how to play it, William."

"Well, you jus' pick sides," said William. "An' then —well you'll soon see how it goes."

They soon saw how it went. William and Ginger picked sides and soon the room was a bedlam of fighting, shouting, scuffling children. Miss Fountain watched with a growing air of mystification.

"Not a very pretty dance," she murmured to her neighbour. "Too modern. No rhythm or harmony. Not at all what I'd expected."

But the Over-Sixties enjoyed it. It was, at any rate, better than 'Break Break, Break,' or the 'Ode on the Death of the Duke of Wellington.' One sprightly old man with mischievous blue eyes and a long humorous mouth joined in the game as a tamer. Two old women, rocking with laughter, concealed a couple of lions behind their chairs while they gathered breath to return to the fray. A sporting-looking old woman who had won ten shillings on the Derby last year laid a bet of sixpence on the final result. The others gave encouragement and advice and cheered both sides indiscriminately. Miss Fountain sat watching in silence, the smile growing more fixed and frozen on her face.

It was Douglas who finally pointed out the time.

"I've got to be goin'," he panted to William. "My mother said I'd got to be home early. I got in a row yesterday for makin' toffee in the coffee machine an' I don't want to get into another today."

"All right. P'raps we'd all better go," said William, pulling his tie round from the back of his neck and drawing his shirt together where the buttons had been torn off.

Fate had so far befriended him, but he knew that Fate was not to be relied on indefinitely. The frozen aspect of Miss Fountain's smile held a warning that could no longer be safely ignored. Better go while the going was good. . . .

"Come on, everybody," he shouted. " 'S time to go now."

Towsled, dishevelled, panting, he led them up to Miss Fountain, baring his teeth in the glassy smile that comprised his "company manners."

"Thank you very much, Miss Fountain. We've had a very nice time, thank you, an' we've got to go now. . . . Come on! " he shouted in authoritative tones to his fellow guests. "Come on, quick! "

They trooped to the door in a straggling chattering crowd. Miss Fountain watched them, paralysed by amazement. Then, as if their departure broke some spell, she leapt to her feet.

"One moment! " she called, hurrying to the door. "One moment, children! "

She stood at the doorway, peering up and down the road. Her guests had vanished into the dusk.

It was after lunch the next day that William, wandering into the kitchen, where his mother and Mrs. Peters were washing-up, heard his mother say:

"And did you enjoy the Over-Sixty Club outing yesterday, Mrs. Peters?"

Mrs. Peters shook her head gloomily as she plunged the tumblers recklessly into the washing-up water.

"Naw," she said. "Sittin' in that there coach got on me nerves an' there weren't nothin' to do at the seaside when you got there. Now my friend what goes to the one over at Hadley 'ad a much better time."

"What did they do there, Mrs. Peters?" asked Mrs. Brown, rescuing a tablespoon that Mrs. Peters had tipped into the chicken bucket along with the mashed potatoes.

"Well, this friend o' mine, she's a bit deaf an' she can never 'ardly 'ear the notices what's given out, but it seems they 'ad a kids' tea party—pore kids from out London way, likely. They give 'em a good tea an' then they all 'ad games. Me friend didn't join in, bein' a bit stiff in 'er joints, like, but she said it were a nice sort o' change, givin' a tea party to pore kids. She enjoyed jus' watchin' of 'em play, 'specially as that there Miss Fountning what was runnin' it 'ad bin a-readin' of po'ms what me friend couldn't 'ear but what they all said she was lucky not bein' able to."

"Oh, yes," said Mrs. Brown. "Miss Fountain . . . She's coming to tea with me today."

"Gosh!" said William in a voice of horror from the doorway.

"What's the matter, dear?" said Mrs. Brown.

"Oh—er—nothin'," said William.

"She's only just come to live in the neighbourhood and
154

I called on her last week. She's very keen on these Over-Sixty Clubs, so they asked her to help with the one in Hadley and she said that she thought that the various local Over-Sixty Clubs should co-operate more and she's coming to tea with me today to discuss it. . . . Will you be in to tea, William?"

"No, I won't," said William firmly.

"All right, dear," smiled Mrs. Brown. "You needn't sound so determined. You'd like her if you met her. She's very nice."

"Yes, I know she is," said William. "I mean, I bet she is. I mean, I've got to go out somewhere very important this afternoon, a long way off, an' I've got to start very early."

His plans, however, miscarried. He wasted an hour or so in the garden, completing the primeval swamp that he was constructing out of the compost heap and the contents of the rain-tub. Then he went upstairs to his bedroom to remove the traces of this occupation and became absorbed in a book called *The Mystery of the Branded Skeleton* that Henry had lent him the evening before . . . so that by the time he crept slowly and silently down the stairs the visitor had already arrived and was ensconced in an arm-chair that commanded a full view of the open sitting-room door.

William hovered in the hall, waiting his opportunity to slip unseen across the open doorway and make good his escape. Miss Fountain's gentle voice floated out to him.

"Yes, I do feel so strongly that we ought to co-operate more closely over these Over-Sixty clubs, Mrs. Brown. Pool ideas and experiences and so on. . . ."

"Yes, of course," said Mrs. Brown, "but I understand that you have a very flourishing one in Hadley. My char-woman was saying that a friend of hers enjoyed yester-day's meeting very much."

155

A strange exression came into Miss Fountain's pleasant face.

"Yesterday . . . Yesterday's was a most extraordinary experience, Mrs. Brown, and I should like to tell you about it."

"Yes, do, Miss Fountain. I agree that it would be very useful to pool our experiences, as you say."

"It was a *most* extraordinary experience, Mrs. Brown, and I still don't understand it. You see, all the other helpers were down with 'flu and I was left to carry on alone and—it was foolish, perhaps—but I thought I'd like to make a sort of *occasion* of it and provide a really enjoyable entertainment. I'd seen some charming child dancers—Miss Mirabel's Juveniles—at a little charity show in London. They did some delightful old-world dances in old-world costumes—minuets and that sort of thing—so I engaged them at my own expense and, again rather foolishly, perhaps, provided a really good tea for them, so that they would be fresh and in good spirits for their dancing. But evidently there was a thick fog in London——"

"Yes, my husband said there was," put in Mrs. Brown.

"—and Miss Mirabel rang up to say that she was afraid they wouldn't be able to get here, but I had one of my *feelings* that they'd come, after all, and my feelings very seldom mislead me. Anyway, I hoped for the best and got everything ready and meantime read some of my favourite Tennyson poems to the dear old people, which they much enjoyed, and then——" Her voice faltered.

"Yes?" Mrs. Brown encouraged her.

"Well, they came. Miss Mirabel's Juveniles. About twenty of them. The costumes had apparently gone astray and Miss Mirabel had not been able to accompany them, but they came. They did full justice to the tea and then——"

Again she stopped.

"Then they danced for you, I hope?" said Mrs. Brown.

"Yes, they danced, Mrs. Brown, but it was such an odd dance. Chaotic. Without rhythm or harmony or beauty. I'm always so sorry to see this chaotic element in modern art and I was quite distressed to see that it had invaded even children's dancing. There was that note of *violence* in it that one finds nowadays in all modern art. However, they carried the dance through to the end and then went away—rather hurriedly and abruptly, I thought. But no doubt they had to catch their train to London, so one must not blame them for that. But this morning—well, I simply can't understand it . . ."

Again Miss Fountain's voice died away into a perplexed murmur. Again Mrs. Brown gently encouraged her.

"Yes, Miss Fountain?"

"Well, I had a letter from Miss Mirabel, saying how sorry she was that her Juveniles had not been able to come. The whole thing is most mysterious. I can't make head or tail of it . . . Of course, as I said, I was disappointed in the children. I don't think they were the same lot of children as I saw before. They were so much less—dainty and graceful. The boy who appeared to be in charge of them——"

William, absorbed by this recital, had inadvisedly advanced to a spot from which he could see and hear without obstruction, and it was at this point that Miss Fountain turned to see him standing in the doorway. She blinked and gulped.

"Oh, come in, William," said Mrs. Brown. "This is my son, William, Miss Fountain . . . Well, say 'how d'you do,' William."

William, his face wearing its most wooden expression, advanced into the room and held out a grubby hand.

"How d'you do," he said hoarsely.

157

Miss Fountain still sat there, blinking and gulping as if in the last stages of suffocation.

"If you'll 'scuse me. I've gotter go now," continued William. "I've gotter go quick."

"But, William—" began Mrs Brown, then stopped.

The figure of William could be seen making its way in headlong flight down to the gate and along the road towards Ginger's house. The net of Fate was closing round him. There would be questions . . . explanations . . . retribution . . . and he wanted to retreat in as good order as possible.

He held a brief consultation with Ginger, then the two set off for the old barn, carrying a sheet of paper. In silence they affixed the sheet of paper to the door with a drawing pin, then hastened towards the woods with the air of those bent rather upon postponing some inevitable catastrophe than merely enjoying the countryside.

The notice fluttered disconsolately in the breeze. It read:

Overtenn klub

The overtenn klub will be klozed til furthur nottis.

cined William Brown.

ARMADA BOOKS

Hundreds of thousands of boys and girls are collecting our wonderful Armada books. At half-a-crown each, Armada books are magnificent entertainment and value. *Always ask your parents and relatives to buy Armada books for your presents.* Just think, you can have four delightful books for only 10/-, eight for one pound! Tell your friends about them. Always ask your newsagent or bookseller for Armada books, but if you have difficulty they may be obtained, price 2s. 9d. each (including postage), from Armada Books, Dorset House, 13a Old Burlington Street, London, W.1.

ARMADA BOOKS *continued*